LITTLE ANN

LITTLE ANN

EMMA CHARLES

This is a work of fiction. Names, characters, places, and incidents either are the product of the author's imagination or are used fictitiously. Any resemblance to actual persons, living or dead, events, or locales is entirely coincidental.

Little Ann. Copyright © 2023 by Flora Church.

www.emmacharles.net

To my mom, Ann Thompson Church,
My first and best reader
Love you always

Chapter 1

fiddlehead

Brushy Creek, Lawrence County, Kentucky

Little Ann sat on the wide, deep front porch shelling peas, her straight-backed rocker pulled well back into the shade. The mid-day sun picked out every leaf on the old mulberry tree in the corner of the yard, reflected back from the dusty lane winding along the creek bottom before disappearing up the hollow, dazzled from the tin roofs of the post office, sawmill, sorghum sheds, and from the harness of the mules in the hillside cornfield. Squinting at the straggling row of her siblings bent over their hoes in that same cornfield, she drew back further into the shade with a small sigh. The rocker beside her stopped its rhythmic creaking.

"Little Ann," Great-uncle Joseph leaned forward to touch her knee, his cloud of fly-away white hair tumbling forward to frame his lined face, "you go on in the house and ask your mama for a cold cloth for your head." He shook her knee gently as she said nothing. "Go on, Little Ann, lie down until it passes."

Stubbornly she fought the oncoming headache, too sick to shake her head.

"I'll go in when we finish, Uncle Joseph."

Her eyes screwed tight now, she lowered her forehead to her clenched fists. Through the waves of nausea, she heard the creak of the screen door, then the measured tread of booted feet and a rustling of skirts. Her grandmother's voice came to her from far away.

"Take her into the front bedroom, Poppy, it'll be cooler there."

Then strong hands lifted her slight figure from the rocker as if she were a lap baby and not a grown woman, or nearly so, for she'd turned thirteen with the first of this year. Inside, her grandfather laid her gently on the bed, and she heard the shades being drawn before her grandmother's skirts rustled again and her fists were pried away from her face long enough for a cold, moist cloth to be pressed over her eyes and temples. Her grandmother stroked her thick, wavy, dark chestnut hair like her mother's, away from her face.

As the pain and nausea subsided, she heard Uncle Joseph's soft voice humming and the creaking of the rocking chair from the front porch.

She woke to a gentle hand on her shoulder, then her mother's soft voice.

"Little Ann, wake up, sissy."

Turning over, she faced her mother's anxious eyes which lightened when she saw that the worst had passed, and although her daughter's face was white and drawn, the pinched look of pain had faded.

"Are you hungry, Little Ann?" At her cautious nod, her mother slipped an arm around her shoulders and helped her stand. "Come out to the kitchen for a bite to eat."

She saw as they came out of the bedroom that it was late, dinner and supper both come and gone, the little ones bathed and put to bed with the middle ones. Now the quiet creak of the swing on the porch and the murmur of low voices told her that older brother John and sister Sarah sat out on the porch with her father, Walter Lee, and the old folks. In the kitchen her mother crumbled left-over cornbread into a tall glass and poured sweet milk from the cooler over it.

"Little Ann, you don't eat more'n that, you'll never get to be big like your mama!" Her daddy grinned at her across the breakfast table. It was an old joke. Mama weren't much bigger, herself, than her second daughter.

"I saw Little Ann riding on a grasshopper just the other day!" John declared, rolling his eyes at his sister. The younger children burst out laughing, and John protested, "She rode half-way up the holler before it stopped to set her down."

"I would've gone further, but I knew you'd miss me," she countered. Emmett and Emeline, the four-year-old twins, nodded anxiously.

"Don't you go 'way, Little Ann."

"Hush, John." Mama sat down at the table. "Eat now, there's work to be done."

Martha, nine years old; then John, fourteen years old; then Albert, eleven years old; Sarah Elizabeth, fifteen years old; then Peter, seven years old; then Little Ann. She counted them off as they hoed corn for yet another hot, bright morning. Emmett and Emmy, she knew, would be somewhere underfoot, most likely on the post office porch while Grandma Emeline took care of the mail. Between Peter and the twins had been another baby, a little boy named Joseph Lee.

Little Ann hoed on steadily, but her eyes followed the line of the ridgetop curving above them. Baby Joseph lay buried up yonder, with all the other Sanders—Aunt Virgie Lou, who had been no older than Little Ann when the influenza had taken her and great-Uncle Samuel, who she could remember only as a tall, thin form, coughing by the fire when he came to visit. The graves of Poppy's mother and father, whose photographs hung in the parlor, and five of Poppy's brothers were up there, too. Poppy and his brother, who they called Uncle Joseph, were the only two of those boys left.

"Little Ann, stop mooning over James Lester and git them weeds chopped!"

"That great lout!" Little Ann snorted at her older brother and chopped furiously at the soil with her hoe. "I am not mooning over James Lester!"

"Hush," Sarah glared at them both, beads of sweat dampening her hairline. "There's work to be done."

"Yes, Mama!" John bobbed his head in mock seriousness, then grinned at Little Ann.

"Don't!" Sarah began sharply, then bit her lip, ducked her head, and bent over her hoe. Next to her, Peter shook her skirt.

"Sarah?"

Little Ann poked her younger brother in the small of his back with her hoe handle.

"Look here, Peter, them weeds're growing back as fast as you chop'em down!"

Peter turned, his blue eyes wide as he surveyed the row behind him. Martha and Alby whooped with laughter. John winked at Peter as Little Ann chopped the weeds he'd missed. Peter turned a sunny smile on his sister and attacked his row, chopping weeds and corn alike.

"Watch me, Little Ann," he crowed, "I'll get them old weeds!"

Over his head, she stared at the back of her elder sister, her heart afraid.

"Mama's carrying again." Sarah whispered miserably to Little Ann in the dark warmth of the bed they shared. In the wan moonlight, Little Ann could just make out the mounds that marked Martha and Emmy in the other bed. Fear clutched at her insides. She shivered.

"She ain't strong enough, Little Ann. I'm so scared for Mama. Why couldn't they just have stopped with Emmett and Emmy?" Silent sobs shook her sister's sturdy frame, and Little Ann clung to her, her mind whirling until Sarah cried herself to sleep.

What comfort could she give her sister? Mama loved Daddy and Daddy loved Mama. Mama's face would go all soft when Daddy pulled her down on his knee and teased her. And she'd seen Daddy many a morning, slipping out of the house early to gather the eggs for Mama, stoke up the fire for her, carry a heavy pail of milk from the barn for her. Bring her an apple from the hillside orchard, a hundred small ways he told her that he loved her.

But having the twins had almost killed Mama. The doctor had told Daddy then that he was a lucky man—lucky that Mama and both babies had survived. Maybe, the horrible thought crossed her mind before she could catch it back, this baby would come too early, like little Joseph Lee, and Mama's life would be spared.

Snow muffled the solemn clop-clop of the horses' hooves along the frozen earth. The wind stung sharply at Little Ann's cheeks and knees, numbing her all the way through, so she did not feel Martha's cold hand in hers as they followed Sarah and John to the top of the ridge. Her daddy walked alone behind the hearse that carried her mother and a baby girl, born too early to survive. Walter Lee looked neither right nor left, moving like the very life within him had been crushed to bits.

As the pine coffin was lowered into the frozen grave, a long shudder knifed between her shoulder blades and she heard, behind her, Alby's muffled sobs. Sarah's eyes never left the coffin, but her oldest sister did not cry, watching with bitter, angry eyes as the first shovel of dirt rattled on the wooden coffin. Martha buried her face against Little Ann's shoulder, before Poppy lifted her into his arms and held her as she wept.

When the grave was mounded high and the reverend had said his piece, the mourners turned gratefully away from the reminder of untimely death and February's wet, clinging snow, and headed back down the ridge to the farmhouse, where the aunts and great-aunts and neighbor women waited with hot food and drink and the little ones, Peter and Emmy and Emmett. Little Ann did not turn with them. She gave no notice that the crowd was departing, but stood unmindful of the cold dampness, staring at the rapidly whitening mound that marked the final resting place of her mother and the baby which had come too early, her head blank, her heart stopped. The whole world might have been whirling away into the snow. She felt herself falling headfirst into that dark emptiness inside the cold, so much like the open grave had seemed before her.

A hand closed firmly on her shoulder and only then did she raise her eyes from her mother's final resting place. Her great-uncle Joseph put his arm around her shoulders and turned her frozen body away from the grave.

"Come back with us," he began, and it seemed to Little Ann that his voice came from a long way off, calling her back from the dead. "Come back before you take sick."

Too late, too late, she might have laughed, because she could feel the cough tickling deep within her, rolling its way out of her lungs, and the high, far-away kiss of the fever on her forehead even in the cold. The pneumonia sapped what strength she had, her grandmother holding her head up so she could sip her broth in the days which followed her mother's funeral. Little Ann didn't care. It was too much effort to care. She wanted only to close her eyes and not feel, to slip away to the peace promised in the words of the family bible.

It was Emmy and Emmett and Peter, though, who brought her back to them, the youngest ones creeping into her sick room each morning, until she finally heard what they were whispering, one little hand on her heart, then another.

"See, Emmy, her heart's beating. Little Ann's not dead like Mama."

Not dead, no, Little Ann thought later, but cold still though the seasons had changed again. A cold hard weight had settled in the hollow where her heart used to beat and the cold chilled her bones so that she moved as if something inside her might break. And worse, no laughter came to warm her—the house silent save for the cold hiss of Sarah's anger. For in the months since the loss of their mother, Sarah's eyes burned with anger whenever her glance rested upon their father and she would not speak to him. Walter Lee seemed not to notice or not to care, working dawn to dusk about the farmstead. When he ate, it was a cold piece of meat and cornbread out in the fields. At supper, more often than not, he took his plate to the porch and ate alone. Miserably, Little Ann watched him go one night, then quickly pushed her plate away and followed after him.

Her daddy sat in a straight-backed chair in the corner of the porch shaded by the lattice with its climbing rose and the spreading branches of the old pear tree. His plate sat empty on his knee. She slipped out the door, careful not to let it slam, and sidled along the wall until she reached her father's chair. She knelt by his knee and covered his rough hand with both of hers and laid her cheek upon her hands. He did not stroke her hair, as he might have done in the past, but neither did he pull his hand away. Little Ann felt a swelling in her heart and she lifted her face to her father.

"Daddy," she whispered, "cain't you love us no more with Mama gone?"

His hand came up to stroke her hair just once.

"Ah, Little Ann," he began, then his voice broke and he reached for her, the plate clattering to the porch floor. Her daddy held her as sobs shook his frame. And when the fit of crying passed, he wiped his face and blew his nose and held her against his chest like he might have held Emmy.

"Lord, how I miss your mama." He was quiet a moment. "I loved her before I knowed it, honey. She came to visit me one day with her cousin Gracie. I was going off to the war, and they came to say good-bye. Jenny Ann were just a big girl then, no older than Sarah. When it got late, I walked them down to the ford in the branch, to see them on their way.

"And your mama, I remember, she was laughing and she looked back to wave at me. All of a sudden, it came to me—there was the girl I was going to marry."

She held her breath, willing him to go on. After a while, he sighed.

"I wrote to her from the war and she answered. And by the time I came home, we had an understanding that we would marry.

"I caught the train to Ashland; it was late. I bought a jar of likker for my daddy and caught a ride in a coal wagon as far up the holler as I could get. I reckon it were two o'clock in the morning when I stood in the lane outside your grandpa's house and wondered if I dared wake them up to see Jenny Ann. I figured old Isaac—Poppy— would skin me alive being disturbed so late of night, so I set off for home instead.

"Granny Sanders lived with us then. She were blind and kept a bed downstairs; ever'body else slept upstairs. I came across the yard in the moonlight, barely crunching the gravel. When I set foot on the first step up to the porch, I heard Granny call out.

"'It's Walter Lee! Walter Lee's come home!' And by the time I got inside, Maw and Paw and all the young'uns was awake. It were the next morning before I got back to your mama.

"She and her sister Sarah Elizabeth were inside when Miz Emeline answered the door. She cried out, one hand to her heart, 'Jenny Ann, Walter Lee's home!' And I heard your mama laughing. 'Sure he is, Mama!' Then Jenny

Ann must have looked out the window, for the next thing I knew, she came flying through that door and I was holding her in my arms, and Lord knows, I kissed her right in front of her mama."

He stopped then and in the silence, Little Ann wiped her eyes and saw her brothers John and Alby on the steps in the moonlight, listening. Emmy sat quietly in John's lap, her thumb in her mouth. Martha stood beside her father's chair, her arms around Peter and Emmett, in his nightshirt. She felt her father draw in a deep breath that came out on a sigh.

"Lord knows I loved your mama, and I never thought to bury her so young. Now you're all I have left of her. Don't you ever think I don't love you."

She slipped from her daddy's lap as John brought Emmy to him and he reached out blindly to embrace the crush of his children—Emmett and Peter crowding onto his lap with Emmy, Martha and Alby wrapping their arms around him, and John holding them all. Little Ann watched, she'd already had her turn, and lifted her eyes to the doorway where Sarah's eyes blazed with contempt.

Liar. Liar. Her sister's voiceless lament sounded loud and clear upon Sarah's face, and she knew what her sister thought. How could their daddy have taken such a chance with Jenny Ann's life? He'd known another pregnancy could be the death of his wife. Sarah turned on her heel without saying a word.

Chapter 2

ginseng

Lying still in the featherbed, Little Ann listened to the rise and fall of Emmy's soft breath beside her. Moonlight flooded the summer bedroom, and she could hear, through screens, the cowbells from the hillside pastures as the cattle moved about. From the second bed across the room came the gentle snuffling snore that marked Martha. Turning on her side and facing the window, she could not see her sister Sarah next to Martha, but some quality of the silence told her that her older sister slept, her back turned to the rest of the bedroom. Miserably, she rubbed at her eyes with the back of her hand. Sarah wanted them all to hate their daddy, as if she thought he'd killed Mama. But Little Ann couldn't—not even to make Sarah happy.

From downstairs came the soft drift of voices where her daddy and grandparents and great-Uncle Joseph sat up keeping company with Aunt Sarah Elizabeth and Uncle James Preston. Aunt Sarah Elizabeth was her mama's older sister. Uncle James Preston worked for the railroad, and he and Aunt Sarah Elizabeth had a fine house in Louisville, away from the hills. She heard her daddy chuckle, and something eased inside her. He'd been going to Fort Gay some nights, coming home late at night smelling of the liquor he couldn't get in Louisa. She pulled her quilt—one of the last Mama had pieced—to her chin and closed her eyes against the moonlight. Crickets chirped, and she felt Emmy stir against her. At last the quilt and the featherbed warmed her, and she slept.

Aunt Sarah Elizabeth tucked into the Sunday fried chicken with both hands, her plate mounded with mashed potatoes and gravy, greens, and the last of their mama's canned corn. Uncle James sat across the table from his wife, John and Alby to either side of him and great-Uncle Joseph next to John with Poppy next to Alby. Sarah sat to the left of their aunt with Martha squeezed next to her oldest sister. Little Ann sat at the far right of her aunt, next to her daddy, who sat in his usual place at the end of the table. Her grandmother Emeline sat where her mother usually sat, opposite her daddy. The three littlest ones were crowded around her grandmother today—Emmy on her lap and the boys squeezed to either side of her.

The cause of this tight squeeze, Vina Jones, sat stolidly in the chair next to Little Ann, overflowing her chair and taking second helpings of Mama's corn, pausing long enough between mouthfuls to praise Emeline's cooking in a low voice. Her daddy hadn't been going to

Fort Gay just for the liquor. She had seen Vina looking around before dinner was on the table, had seen the way she noticed the lace curtains at the windows and the thick rug on the floor in the front parlor. The woman's eyes had narrowed at the sight of Mama's Blue Willow china, the heavy, good furniture, the walnut staircase as it turned to the upstairs landing, the carved mantelpiece upon which rested two cut glass lanterns, a green glass candy dish, Mama's china birds, and the photograph of her parents on their wedding day. In the photograph, her mama was seated and wore a dark green dress, her auburn hair pinned up and glowing. Walter Lee stood behind her, his hand resting on her shoulder. Her mama had reached up to cover his hand with hers; both seemed pleased and a little grin escaped her daddy.

Winfrey Adams had the softest hands Little Ann had ever seen on a man—young or old. His large hands at the end of thin wrists seemed too long for his shirtsleeves. These were buttoned at the cuffs and he wore black suspenders against his white shirt and dark blue trousers. His heavy black shoes were coated with dust, where he'd ridden his mare up the dry holler from the main road to Louisa. His suit jacket of dark gray tweed showed a bulge in the left breast pocket where he carried his pipe. He was nineteen years old, a high school graduate, and clerked for his Uncle Raymond at the bank in Louisa.

Although the air was cool, Sarah Elizabeth and Winfrey sat out on the porch in the swing, talking in low voices. Great-uncle Joseph sat in a wicker rocker on the other end of the porch, reading his bible and rocking slowly. Every time the rocker stopped, Winfrey would push his brown waves out of his eyes, followed by a short "A-hem" as he cleared his throat. Little Ann, sitting in the front room on the sofa, suppressed a smile. Great-uncle Joseph might be close to ninety years old, but that didn't mean he'd lost his sense of humor. Beside her, her grandmother paused in her darning and chuckled, but all she said was, "Your stitches are right nice. Cain't tell your work from your Mama's."

Little Ann looked down at the half-pieced quilt block in her lap. Her daddy had taken some of the tobacco money from last year's crop and driven Mama into the store at Blaine, where she'd picked out bright calicos for a pieced quilt top. She had helped her mama cut out all the pieces, but the quilt top had never gotten finished after old Doc Carter ordered her mama to her bed if she hoped to carry that last baby to term. She picked up the next piece and laid it in place, her needle moving in and out. Even bedrest hadn't been enough to save her mama or the child she carried. The needle pricked her finger and she sighed. Best to pay attention. She had a mind to finish her mama's last quilt for Sarah, as a wedding present, even if her older sister was looking mighty pleased with herself.

"Winfrey's gonna get a job clerking for the railroad. Uncle James Preston said he'd help him. We're gonna move to Louisville soon's we can, and I'm gonna have as nice a house as Aunt Sarah Elizabeth." Sarah didn't mind talking to her sister now, as long as the whole conversation was about Sarah and how she was leaving the holler as soon as she could. She'd prattled on and on about Winfrey and the life they would have together as Little Ann had pressed her sister's nicest blouse before Sunday dinner and Winfrey's arrival.

Out on the porch the rocker paused again, and right on cue came "A-hem." She might have giggled, but the thought of her sister leaving hurt her heart. First Mama, soon Sarah, and although Sarah was getting married, it felt like she might as well have died when Mama did. This Sarah had turned her face and heart away from her family and all her care was centered on her own wants and comforts. It wouldn't be long now before Winfrey asked their daddy for Sarah. Her sister would be seventeen in three months' time—their daddy wouldn't deny her.

Chapter 3

chiggers

Tipping the basin of soapy water down the drain, Little Ann's daddy stood for a moment, his eyes drawn to the sight of the wagon pulling out into the lane that ran in front of the farmhouse—between the yard and the creek. Then he reached for his coat and met his daughter's gaze.

"We'll be back before dark, Little Ann. Best if you feed the young'uns early and have our supper waiting. No doubt them boys'll be hungry."

Her daddy didn't wait for an answer, but strode out the kitchen door and across the porch. He didn't look back as Emmy burst into sobs and buried her face in her older sister's skirts. Little Ann watched as he mounted his horse and rode out, following the wagon carrying her grandparents and Great-uncle Joseph and all their belongings to a snug little house in Louisa. When he returned, the wagon would be full again—but this time it would be bringing Vina Jones and her two sons—Estil and Robert, called Poke, and their household goods here, to her mother's home. Only she wouldn't be Vina Jones any longer, not once her daddy married that woman before the justice of peace at the Lawrence County courthouse in Louisa.

She couldn't blame her grandparents for leaving. The house had always been overflowing with family, but there wasn't room to add three more people. Since her mother's untimely death, it had been a blessing to have her grandmother here to help tend to the little ones and the house. But her grandmother's tight lips had told her all she needed to know about Vina Jones. That and the fierce hug and whispered words before she'd climbed into the wagon. "Lordy, Lordy, Little Ann! You have to be strong now, girl, like your blessed mama was. It ain't going to be easy on you all. See to them little ones as best you can." She'd looked away for a moment. "Lord knows, we won't be able to do much to help you'uns from Louisa." By moving into their home in town, her grandparents had lost the little they'd earned in renting the place. But Little Ann knew it wasn't the money her grandmother meant. Watching the wagon head down the lane, she wanted to chase after it, hold it back, toss her siblings and herself into the back of it, then holler "Go!" Now she sighed. The worst thing, she thought, was how her daddy looked as he set off. Not an ounce of joy in what he was about to do. Then, why? Why bring another woman into her mama's home?

"Hush, Emmy," she patted her sister's back. "You find Emmett and go out to the henhouse for me. Can you make them ole hens give you two eggs? I'm thinking I can bake us a cake for supper."

As Emmy ran out the door, hollering for her brother, Little Ann walked swiftly into the parlor. Martha and the other boys were nowhere to be seen. Martha had looked as if their daddy had smacked her when he told them over breakfast that he was marrying that woman and that they needed to help their grandparents load the wagon. Then her younger sister screamed at him. "You cain't! You cain't do that to us!" Sobbing, she'd pushed her chair away from the table and run through the house and up the stairs to their bedroom, slamming the door behind her. The twins, eyes wide in fright, set to howling, "No, Daddy! We don't want a new mama! Daddy, we don't want no other mama!" Peter's eyes filled with tears and little whimpers of distress escaped him, he pushed his fist hard against his mouth and gulped.

"You'uns hush up that squalling or you'll get a whipping!" Their daddy stood, nearly overturning his chair, and strode out of the kitchen, the screen door banging shut behind him.

John pushed aside his plate and went outside in long loping strides, but instead of confronting his father, she saw him go to his grandparents and Great-uncle Joseph. Alby set his glass of milk down blindly and followed his brother outside to the wagon. The twins and Peter crowded around Little Ann, bawling. She helped them dry their eyes.

"You won't leave us, Little Ann?" They begged, and when she reassured them, "You promise? Cross your heart, Little Ann?"

"Yes," she hugged them all to her. "I promise. Jest as long as you need me, I won't leave you."

Now she wiped her tears at the memory, and looked about her. She wanted no eyes to see what she was about, no one to tell tales if questions were asked. Quickly she gathered up the photograph of her parents, the delicate, green carnival glass candy dish her daddy had won for her mama at the county fair the year John was born, and pursed her lips at the china birds. Those she would sacrifice, there wasn't room to hide everything her mama cherished. In the kitchen, she selected two worn dish-towels and wrapped her treasures carefully. These she carried upstairs to the smallest of the summer bedrooms and laid them on the dresser before she tugged the bed-stead away from the wall. Beneath the bed, a loose floor-board came up easily. Little Ann stowed her prizes away and bit her lip against the bitter tears that threatened to fall. Putting the bed to rights once more, she hastened down to the kitchen just as Emmy and Emmett and Peter trooped in, Emmy carrying the egg basket.

"Look, Little Ann, we got three eggs!"

If Little Ann thought baking a cake would ease the tension when her daddy came home that evening, she found instead that it showed her worst fears come to life. Her daddy was bleary-eyed and staggering when he ushered Vina into the house, her overgrown sons leering behind him. Vina and her sons took generous double helpings of everything on the table at supper, including the cake. Little Ann managed to split one piece into three for Peter and the twins, who hadn't said a word all through the meal. Alby had disappeared during the afternoon and hadn't come back for supper. Little Ann slipped a triangle of cornbread into her apron pocket to carry upstairs to Martha after the supper dishes were washed.

When the little ones were asleep, Little Ann crawled into bed beside Martha. Her sister grunted and turned over to face her.

"I'll run away, Little Ann," she whispered. "I purely hate that woman!"

"Hush," Little Ann consoled the younger girl. "You've got school, you won't have to be around her all the time."

Chapter 4

copperhead

"Here," Ann thrust the brown paper sack at her brother. "Go on, take it, John!" she whispered, her throat aching at yet another loss. "Them's two biscuits I saved you from last night's supper and some of this morning's bacon." Her eyes flicked to the pan on the stove. "We got enough for us." There wasn't, of course. There was never enough to feed them all now; Vina's two sons took their share and more before she could even try to see that Peter and the twins were served. And Vina, heavily pregnant, ate like a fattening hog.

"What's this?" John had opened the bag and was peering at something in the bottom of the bag, wrapped in newspaper under the biscuits.

"Mama's china bird." John's mouth tightened. "Aunt Polly always liked them china birds. Tell her the other one ... the other one got broke." John's fist clenched, and she laid her hand on his arm. "Last night, after supper, when you was gone. Estil did it; he blamed Alby. Alby got in a good lick at him, though. Daddy was passed out by then. I reckon Estil'll have a shiner this morning." And Alby'd earned himself a trip to the woodshed as soon as Vina went whining to Walter Lee this morning, but she didn't say that out loud.

John grinned a little at the thought of Alby, and then shook his head.

"I gotta go before Daddy gets up. I ain't arguing or fussing with him no more. Uncle Henry's said if I earn my keep, I can stay with him and Aunt Polly. I'd take you all with me, but you know Uncle Henry's already got enough mouths to feed." He gave his sister an awkward half-hug, and then stopped at the edge of the porch. "I cain't do much to help you all, but I'll be at church most Sundays if...."

Little Ann watched until her brother's tall form rounded the post office and disappeared up the lane. He was a spitting image of their daddy, she thought. Same lanky, muscular build, a head of dark curls, brown eyes, and a thin, square-jawed face like all the Sanders men.

Facing off, yesterday, like a near mirrored image of each other, angry, fists drawn. But where John had stood tall, his daddy had stumbled, drunk already on corn likker. Then her brother had turned away in disgust and strode away from the farm. He'd crept back this morning to say good-bye. Now he was gone with nothing but the clothes on his back, two cold biscuits, and Mama's china bird.

Standing at the sink, filling the coffeepot with water, Little Ann looked out the window and the images filled her mind again of yesterday, the sight of her brother John coming at a dead run down the path from the upper pasture. Dropping her dishrag, she'd hurried from the kitchen. As she passed the henhouse, she could hear John shouting and then she saw him, bent over a huddled form on the ground outside the outhouse.

"It's okay, Peter, it's okay. They's gone."

John met his sister's eyes and shook his head. Together, they helped Peter stand and got his overalls pulled up and snapped. The backs of the boy's pale legs were a mass of thin red welts, some bleeding. His face was blotched with tears and snot and dirt from the path. She used her apron to wipe his face clean, then he buried his head against John's shoulder, his thin arms tight around his brother's neck as John picked him up and held him.

"I was in the pasture up back of the house, mending fences and I saw them two devils laughing down by the outhouse. I thought they was after one of the dogs again, but it were Peter." Their younger brother's sobs had quieted now, and John went on in a low voice. "They must have caught him coming out of the outhouse. You know it's hard for Peter to get the straps of his overalls hooked by hisself."

She nodded and stroked her younger brother's hair.

"Estil and Poke each had a willow switch," John swallowed hard. "They was taking it time about tripping him and pushing him down, while the other one whipped his bare legs with a switch.

"I'll kill them sons a bitches, I get ahold of them. They ran off like cur dogs when they saw me coming."

At the kitchen porch they were met by Vina, Estil and Poke crowded behind her, and their father listening to Vina's high whining voice. Through the screen door behind them, she could see Martha and Alby with the twins in the kitchen. Good—she hoped Martha had the sense to feed the little ones while their stepmother's back was turned. Vina was wagging a finger at John, the other hand cupping her great belly.

"I won't have you telling lies all the time on my boys, not in my own home, John Sanders."

Estil nudged his brother.

"No sir, Mr. Sanders, sir. We just got home ourselves. Why, we been down the road helping Mr. Skaggs all after-noon. You know he's got that bad back." Poke nodded. "Did poor little Peter hurt hisself?"

John set Peter down and the little boy took Little Ann's hand and hid his face in her skirts. Walter Lee came down the steps, staggering as he did so, and faced his oldest son.

"I've had enough of all your fussing, John. Ever'day. Just fussing and scrapping and commotion. As long as you live under my roof, you'll do what I say, boy! Or I'll haul you out to the woodshed, see if I don't."

John's face twisted. He looked past his father, swaying in front of him.

"You two's lower than tits on a boar hog and just as worthless," John spat. "You lay another hand on one of my family and you'll answer to me." He turned on his heel then and stalked off down to the road, turned up it and kept going without a backward glance.

"Well," Vina's thin lips set in a hard line. "Help me inside, boys. Supper's on the table."

"Yes, Mama."

Walter Lee followed them in without a backward glance where she stood with Peter.

Lifting her brother, she carried him around to the front porch where she could slip inside and upstairs with him. Martha came into the bedroom they all shared now as she dipped a cloth in the wash basin to bathe the little boy.

"Here," Martha held out a half glass of cold milk and fetched a biscuit with a bit of pork chop from her apron pocket. "It's the rest of my supper—all I could bring without *her* seeing me."

"Stay with him, Martha. I'll have Alby bring Emmy and Emmett up. Keep the little ones up here. You know I've got to clear up the kitchen." If she was lucky, there might be a biscuit or two left for her own supper.

Her arms full of clean sheets and the children's clean clothes, Little Ann felt for the doorknob to their bedroom. The door stuck fast and wouldn't open.

"Who's there?"

"Martha Sanders, open this door. It's me, Ann."

There was a scraping sound, as of a chair being pulled away from the door, then Martha opened it just wide enough for her to slip inside. Quickly, Martha shut the door and pushed the chair back under the door knob.

"What on earth?"

Martha's schoolbooks were strewn across one bed, paper and a pencil lay where she'd tossed them. Martha took the load of laundry from her sister's arms and set it atop the chest of drawers next to the bed.

"I'm right sorry that I left you with all the washing. But I have a history test tomorrow and Miss Hillis wants an essay for English class on what a high school education means to us. I'm going to high school in the fall, Little Ann. I am." Her sister's voice was escaping like steam from the wash kettles. "I'm not staying here taking care of any more young'uns that woman has. I'll bet she's already carryin' again." Martha snorted. "You're like a slave, Little Ann, cleaning and cooking all day long. That fat cow Daddy married doesn't lift a finger around here. I swear, she's gonna work us all to death.

"And that Poke—" Martha shuddered and dropped her voice lower. "He gives me the creeps. Every time I turn around, he's always watching me." As she talked, she opened drawers and put away clothing, while her sister stripped bedding from the other beds in the room and listened.

"You got to help me," her sister's voice shook. "Sarah won't let me come live with her and Winfrey. I wrote her a letter and asked. She's just 'so busy with church and she volunteers at the library....'" Martha's voice dripped with sarcasm as she quoted Sarah's answer. "And John's gone. And Daddy cain't git his head out of a jar of white lightning long enough to care what happens to me."

Little Ann stepped off the road as a vehicle came up behind her. The car slowed and stopped.

"You going into the store at Blaine, Little Ann?" It was Miss Hillis, the schoolteacher. "I'm on my way to Louisa, I could give you a ride. It wouldn't be much out of my way."

"Thank you, Ma'am, but I'm going to Louisa to see my grandparents."

Miss Hillis smiled.

"Well then, you climb in here beside me and we'll have us a nice visit." As she climbed in the car, the teacher continued. "I'm going to the library in Louisa. If you'd like, I can give you a ride back after your visit."

Little Ann couldn't believe her luck. She'd left a note for Martha telling her that she was going into Louisa and wouldn't be home until late. A pan of oatmeal was covered on the stove with a plate of bacon and a pan of biscuits for breakfast, and she'd sliced ham and left it in the refrigerator with a bowl of coleslaw and a pan of fried potatoes for dinner. Vina Jones—she couldn't bring herself to think of the woman as a Sanders—would have to take care of baby Earl by herself for a day. But with a ride into town and back, she could finish her errand and be home well before dinner.

Her grandmother had made a gingerbread cake— Poppy's favorite—and the tiny house smelled heavenly. Little Ann ate her slice of cake and used her fork to pick up every crumb on her plate. Poppy smiled and took himself and his pipe off to a rocker on the front porch. Emeline, her grandmother, looked around the tidy dining room and sighed.

"I knowed it would be bad, but I never thought that woman...." she sighed. "Truth to tell, I have never liked her. She was mean and lazy even as a girl. I remember her mother, Perlina Jones, who was no better than she should be." Her grandmother sighed again.

"There's me and Poppy in the front bedroom, Joseph in the bedroom behind us, and Miss Hattie has the third bedroom. But you tell Martha that we will put a cot for her in Joseph's room, if she will mind me and work hard in school.

"Joseph mostly sleeps now," her grandmother went on, "poor old soul. Martha could read to him, if she will. He misses his bible and I cain't hardly make out that tiny print no more."

Miss Hattie Edwards nodded vaguely from the living room, where she sat knitting in a rocker before the front window.

"I know you don't have much room, Grandma, and I'm glad you have room for Miss Hattie. I used to see her all the time at the library when Miss Ellen was the librarian. She sat there all day long, just like that." The Misses Edwards had shared a set of rented rooms until Miss Ellen's heart had given out on her one day, and the land-lord hadn't wanted the responsibility of caring for Miss

Hattie. So she'd come to Little Ann's grandparents, and she knew they were glad of the money the old woman paid for her keep.

A car horn sounded outside and she saw her grandfather start down the porch steps. "That's Miss Hillis. She's giving me a ride back up the holler. I told her why I was coming here today, Grandma, and she's offered to bring Martha into town a week from Saturday. Miss Hillis says she'll give Martha enough work to finish the school year and if she does it all, she'll be able to start high school in the fall."

Emeline walked with her granddaughter out to the car and hugged her.

"What does Walter Lee say about Martha coming to live in Louisa?"

She paused at the car. "He doesn't know, Grandma. He probably won't notice when she's gone."

Sarah, John, and Martha. And most of all and hardest of all, her mother. Little Ann buried her face in her pillow that night, so that her crying wouldn't wake the others. Her daddy didn't seem to notice much that went on any more. He spent most of his days up on the ridge; she thought he was running a still up there, helped by Estil and Poke. The farm didn't seem to matter to him, now that John wasn't around to keep things going. She dried her eyes on the corner of her pillowcase. Alby would be next to go, she thought, he was like a dog that had been kicked once too often—the next time he would bite back and then he'd have to go. Some of their kin would probably give him a place to stay—like his brother John, Alby was a hard worker. And that left Peter, sweet, sunny, Peter, and Emmy and Emmett. She'd wracked her brains over and over trying to think of how she could get them away from Vina's slaps and scolds—someplace where there'd be enough food and someone who would love them. About herself, and where she might go—how she might someday have a life of her own—she couldn't even think.

Chapter 5

polecat

The wind whipped the sheets back into Little Ann's face as she pegged the last of the towels to the line and reached for a diaper. Before she finished, the second line was hung with diapers. Rubbing her aching back, she picked up the laundry baskets and made her way into the kitchen.

"Earl, stop that this minute," she smacked at the three-year-old's hand before he could pinch his sister Ruthie's leg again where she sat squalling in a high chair, bits of egg and sausage squished in her fat hands and in her blond curls, her face red and blotchy as she screamed. Emmy stood on a chair at the sink, washing the breakfast dishes as Emmett dried and put them away.

"Lordy, Little Ann!" Vina's querulous voice rose over the noise from where she sprawled on the sofa in the living room, "How many times do I have to tell you to keep them young'uns quiet? Them twins don't leave them little ones alone, they's going to get a right caning this time! Come take this child. James Lee's starting to fuss, he's finished suckling and he needs changing and a bath."

Emmett turned to his older sister and shrugged. She could see for herself what all the fussing in the kitchen was about.

"Go, quick, Emmett, feed the hens and see if there's any eggs before you two get to school. Emmy, you go with him."

Anything to get them out of the house before Vina could get ahold of them. She washed the last skillet, put it in the dishrack and drained the sink, then wiped Ruthie's face and hands and set her down.

"Earl, you come here to Mama, I got a special treat for you!" Vina called. "Little Ann, what on earth's taking you so long? I swear your Mama raised the laziest bunch of girls I ever seen! Why, that ungrateful Miss Uppity Sarah what won't give a dime to her poor ole father and that spiteful Martha telling all them lies in Louisy, don't think I don't hear...." She let it all wash over her as she followed Earl into the living room and carried in Ruthie, who squealed when she saw the rolled candy in her mother's hand. Vina sat in the middle of the sofa, handing off her newest offspring with one hand as she patted the cushion beside her with the other.

"Climb up here by Mama," she cooed to Earl, "who's my sweet boy?" Ruthie latched onto her mother's knee with one hand and flailed her other hand, trying to catch hold of the candy. With three babies in as many years, Vina had put on a mound of weight, her round face weighed by two hefty chins, and her eyes, small and narrow to start with, were by now nearly invisible except when she opened them wide to exclaim over the stupidity of Jenny Ann's children.

Returning to the kitchen, she lay a clean cloth over the kitchen table and put James Lee down in the middle of it. Now there were only the twins and herself of Jenny Ann's children left at the farm. Alby had disappeared one night after supper shortly after Martha had gone to live with their grandparents. He hadn't even said good-bye to her. Taking a basin of warm water to the table, she bit her lip to keep the tears back. Last Sunday, at church, John had taken her aside after the services.

"Nancy Jane and I are getting married in Louisa to-morrow," he'd told her. "Poppy and Grandma Emeline are having us to dinner afterwards, so I'll get to see Martha and Alby, too, if he's not working somewhere in town. Last I heard he was stocking at the Five & Dime store. Grandma Emeline's let him stay with her now that Uncle Joseph's passed on. Him and Martha." Her brother swallowed and looked away for a moment before walking with her outside, away from the other churchgoers. "Nancy Jane's grand-daddy bought the old Miller place last year when it come up for sale. He said we can have it if I can make a go of it. We aim to try. Nancy Jane's a hard worker."

She nodded. "I know she is, and I know she's been sweet on you a long time."

Her brother looked pleased and tried to hide a little grin. He lowered his voice as people walked by. "We got the farmhouse cleaned and Uncle Henry and Aunt Polly give us a bed they had in the barn, and Nancy Jane's family's helped us out with a table and chairs and a sofa. Don't say nothing to Daddy, but we're gonna come up Brushy on our way home from Louisa. You watch for us and have Peter down by the post office. Nancy Jane and I are gonna take him home with us."

"On your wedding night?" She smiled.

"For good." Her brother swallowed hard. "I ain't leaving him with that she-witch and her devil sons a minute longer, I just wish we could take the twins, too, and you, Little Ann. But we won't have much for a while yet, and Peter's big enough to be a help to us."

"He'd work hisself to death for you if you asked him, John."

"He won't have to." He paused as another trickle of churchgoers walked past them and nodded at an acquaintance. "Uncle Henry's got a little beagle 'bout to have a litter of pups any time. I reckon he'll let us have one for Peter, so's he won't miss the twins too much.

"Well, I got to get on. You have Peter by the post office and me and the missus will see you in church next Sunday, God willing."

It hadn't been hard at all to set the twins to their lessons in the kitchen after supper, then walk Peter down to the post office the next day. With the evening meal over, her daddy had commenced drinking and shortly after, snoring, on the sofa in the living room. Vina listened to the radio with a platter of home-made fudge next to her that Little Ann had made earlier. Ruthie and Earl sat at their mother's feet, content to sit still as long as Vina continued to feed the two of them bits of candy. The baby was in his cradle, asleep at least until the fudge ran out and Earl commenced being Earl again.

Peter squirmed on the post office steps next to his sister. The small one room building sat at the corner of the lane, with a big bell on the porch for letting everyone know when the mail had come and been sorted. Her great-grandpa—Grandma Emeline's daddy—had been the postmaster when she was born, and then her grandmother had been given the post when he'd retired. It had been a sore loss, she knew, when her grandmother had moved back to Louisa. The old woman had enjoyed her work—loved handing out the mail and visiting with everybody as they drove up or walked in or rode in to collect their letters and bills and packages. Miss Marthy Pack had been given the job, but the mail had come early in the day, and no one would mind them sitting on the porch.

She slid her hand into her apron pocket and took out a small package of waxed paper.

"Look here, I saved us some candy. Would you like a piece?"

Peter's thin face lit up and he nodded quickly. "Like Mama used to make us? Yes, please!" He sat still and bit carefully into the piece she handed him, looking around him warily.

"It's okay," she told him, putting an arm around her brother and squeezing his shoulders. "It's just you and me."

"Why'd I have to get a bath tonight before supper?" Peter's face was scrubbed shiny, and his dark blond hair stood up at the front in a cowlick. He smiled at her. "You know what? This is my favorite candy. Mama used to let me crack the walnuts with a rock when she made fudge." He stopped to nibble at his candy. "Once I found a cricket under a rock, Little Ann. But it hopped away. Do you think there's enough candy for Emmy and Emmett and another piece for me? Hey," he jumped up, "I'll run up to the house and get Emmy and Emmett. I'll be quick and nobody at all will see me."

She took his arm and guided him back to the step.

"There's some for them, too, for later. You sit here a bit with me."

Her brother sat quietly, taking small bites of his piece of candy. He peered around her.

"What's in that poke there beside you? Do you need me to take it to somebody for you? I can do it. I promise I won't get dirty." She smiled and hugged him close as he finished his candy and relaxed against her.

"Listen, Peter, do you hear someone coming down the road?"

Peter cocked his head and shaded his eyes with his hand, standing up to peer down the lane. "It's a wagon.

Someone's coming in a wagon. Them's Mr. Short's white mules pulling the wagon. When I'm all growed, I'd like to have me some mules just like them." He watched with interest as the wagon pulled to a stop near the post office. And then he was leaping down the steps, inarticulate cries and whimpers of disbelief and joy escaping him, and John was lifting him in a great hug. Nancy Jane reached down from the wagon seat to take Little Ann's hand. Her pale blonde hair fell in soft waves to her chin, and she wore her Sunday best dress of dark blue with a lacy, scalloped white shawl across her shoulders. Tears sparkled unshed in her eyes as she took in the sight of Peter's face buried in the crook of John's neck.

Little Ann offered up her package of fudge and the paper sack in which she had placed Peter's only change of clothes and his winter coat.

"Peanut butter fudge, Nancy Jane, with black walnuts. John's got a mighty big sweet tooth."

John's bride looked at her new husband swinging his brother up onto the wagon seat next to her.

"And a mighty big heart," she said softly. Nancy Jane put her arm around Peter, and John giddyapped to the mules.

With James Lee now washed, dressed, and burped, Little Ann laid him in his cradle in the living room. His mother was nowhere to be seen. Probably, she snorted to herself, Vina had waddled off to her bedroom to take a nap. She snorted again. With any luck, the woman wouldn't get up again before lunchtime, unless the baby needed to be fed. Outside, she checked the laundry she'd hung on the clothesline. She'd unpegged the diapers, but the sheets weren't quite dry enough to take inside, when she saw Emmett coming out of the henhouse with a basket of eggs.

"Where's Emmy?" she demanded, holding her basket to one side and opening the kitchen door for her little brother. He shrugged his shoulders so high, one of his overall straps fell off his shoulder. "You'uns need to get along to school. Miss Hillis don't like you being tardy. Well, where's Emmy?"

"He tole me not to tell, or he'd whomp me good." Emmett whined as he set his eggs on the table. "He tole Emmy he needed her help."

She dropped her basket of laundry and knelt before Emmett, shaking him slightly. "Who, Emmett? Who told you not to tell?"

"It were Poke. He said I'd be whipped if I tole. You know he'll tell Daddy and Daddy'll make me cut a switch." His lower lip trembled.

She dropped his arms. "Where'd Poke take your sister?"

"They was going towards the barn."

"You run and get your schoolbooks and Emmy's too and wait down by the branch for her. When she comes, you take her and get straight to school. You hear me? Don't wait for me."

As her brother set off at a run, she hurried out into the side yard and darted into the shed where her daddy had once butchered hogs. Inside the door, hanging from a nail, was the big old knife John had called the 'hog sticker.' Setting off for the barn, she held the knife in the folds of her skirt, and eased herself around the wide opened doors. Eyes adjusted to the gloom, she took a cautious step forward and then paused when she heard Emmy's soft, gulping sobs and Poke's voice, low and wheedling.

"Don't be a crybaby. You's such a pretty little thing, Emmy. You's so big now. Why, Ole Poke won't hurt you, you gonna like this, it feels so good."

They were in the furthest stall, Emmy backed into a corner against the feeding trough and Poke on his knees before her, his big hands fumbling at the little girl's skirt.

"You git away from her now, Poke Jones."

He lumbered to his feet, a slow grin spreading across his broad face as he saw who it was.

"Come here to me, Emmy," she commanded, and Emmy slipped past Poke and came to her sister, hic-coughing sobs escaping her and her eyes wide with fear. "You run now, fast as you can. Emmett's waiting for you by the branch. You git on to school." Not taking her eyes from Poke, she gave her sister a slight shove in the middle of her back, propelling the little girl forward. "Go on, Emmy, run!" As her sister ran out of the barn, Poke took a step towards her.

"This is more like it," he drawled. "I reckon you and me can be right private here." He took another step forward, stopping short with both hands up as she lifted the hog sticker from her skirts.

"Hey, hey now, no call for that!"

"You try anything with Emmy again, and I'll gut you just like one of Daddy's hogs."

"You too little, girl!" He jeered. "Come on, now, you ruined my fun with that sweet little bit of your sister. You owe me." He lunged for her, but she was quicker. She hadn't rolled and tumbled like a pack of wild pups with John and Alby for nothing. The hog sticker pricked him just above the elbow, drawing blood, and he yelped in surprise, staggered away from her, and grabbed his arm.

"You meaner than a black snake, Little Ann! You skinny little bitch!" He sidled past her, paused at the barn door to fling over his shoulder. "Estil'll fix you. See if he don't!" Then he was off at a loping run towards the lane, holding his arm as he ran.

Chapter 6

Little Ann stood by the counter in the country store at Blaine and waited while tall, thin Mr. O'Bryant assisted a customer. When the woman had left, he turned his bald head to her and smiled.

"What can I get for you today, Little Ann?"

"Please, Mr. O'Bryant, I need to call my grandmother, Emeline Thompson, there at Louisa."

"You look more like your mama ever' day." Mr. O'Bryant moved slowly out from behind the counter and led the way to the telephone box on the wall at the back of the store. "Your mama sure was a fine woman."

"Yes, sir, Mr. O'Bryant, she surely was."

"When you've finished your call, you just hang up the receiver like this."

"Thank you, Mr. O'Bryant."

Emeline was short and to the point.

"I got your letter, Little Ann. I can't talk now, Poppy's feeling poorly, but you'uns coming to the dinner on the ground Sunday?"

"Yes'm."

"Then we'll all see you'uns there, Little Ann."

Dinner on the ground meant a picnic on the church lawn after Sunday services. Little Ann went to the Freewill Baptist Church where her mother's family were members as often as she could manage, taking her younger siblings with her. Vina had objected at first, seeing as how she was a member of the Church of God holy rollers. She'd wanted them all to go to her church or to none at all. But her daddy hadn't cared who went to church or where they went, as long as no one tried to make him go to services and he was left in peace with a jar of likker on Sundays.

With Great-uncle Joseph buried not long after Ruthie was born, and Poppy feeling poorly, she grasped at the hope her grandmother's words had given her. 'We'll *all* see you'uns'—who would be bringing her grandmother to church on Brushy? It wasn't just Poppy's illness that had made Emeline so quick on the telephone. Everyone knew Luella Borders, who ran the telephone exchange in Louisa, was the biggest gossip in all of Lawrence County and neighboring Johnson County, too. Anything she heard on the telephone line was spread far and wide. She was even known to put her two cents' worth into calls that should have been private. The fact that Poppy wasn't feeling well would be told and retold. If her grandmother had anything else to say about her letter, she clearly meant to wait until Sunday.

When Sunday morning came, Little Ann took a peach pie from the back of the pantry where she'd hidden it in a bucket to keep Earl or Ruthie or their older brothers from finding it. Vina had already left for the Pentecostal services with her younger brood, riding with a family from over on Stone Coal Branch. With the twins beside her, she headed for her own church, praying every step of the way.

"Look, look! Grandma's here!" Emmy squealed as they entered the white clapboard church. She let go her sister's hand to run to the pew where her grandmother sat tall and straight next to Sarah, with her brother hurrying right behind her. Winfrey, who was seated at the end of the pew, stood up to let them pass.

After the service and a plate full of food, Sarah was moving from group to group now, exchanging news and pleasantries, Winfrey towed along in her wake, shaking hands with family and friends. The younger kids were having a game with some of their friends from school. Little Ann waved at Nancy Jane, who sat with her parents and John at another table.

"She'll have that baby before New Year's," Grandma Emeline announced, following Little Ann's gaze. "Way she's carrying so low, it'll be a boy, you wait and see." The old woman turned back to her granddaughter and tapped her hand.

"About the twins—I have talked it over with Poppy and he is agreed with me. You know the dear Lord only saw fit to grace us with your Mama and your Uncle

Henry. Henry's doing fine, we give him the farm when he married and we stayed in our house in Louisa till your mama married and needed us." Her grandmother looked away for a moment, her attention caught by a crow of triumph from Peter. "I wrote a letter to Sarah and offered to leave her the house in Louisa after me and Poppy have passed, if she and Winfrey could find it in their hearts to take the twins to raise them up like their own." She shook her head, not a silver hair escaping the tight bun on the top of her head, and sniffed. "Your sister wrote back right quick, saying she would come to Sunday services and take both children home with her. She knowed it were better than coming out to Brushy."

"Grandma—" She felt tears come to her eyes.

"Hush, child. I figured that girl would do her Christian duty if I offered her something to make it worth her while." Her grandmother smiled and gave Little Ann's arm a gentle shake. "You know Winfrey, he's got a good heart. It were a pity Sarah won't give that man children of his own."

"Hello, Miz Thompson." It was Nancy Jane, who waved away a seat. "I need to stand a bit and walk around, thank you kindly. My back is sorely aching." She shifted on her feet, one hand on her bulging stomach. "Little Ann, you remember my cousin Will Short?" Moving aside, she gestured at the young man who stood behind her, hat in his hands, a faint blush washing over his cheeks. "His folks just moved back here from Paintsville."

"Miz Thompson, Ann," he stammered his respects, his brown hair brushed back from his forehead, a bit of curl threatening to fall forward. "I just wanted to say, Ann, that they tole me it was you who brung that peach pie today. It's mighty good." He looked down at the ground, avoiding her grandmother's gaze, and cleared his throat. "Would you have a mind to take a glass of lemonade with me?"

Grandma Emeline answered for her.

"You git along, Little Ann. I'm going to see if there's any of that peach pie left. Poppy's always been partial to peach pie. Mighty nice to see you again, Will. Tell your mama and daddy I was asking after them."

Chapter 7

black snake

The floorboards of the summer bedroom were still warm under Little Ann's bare feet. She poured the last of the hot water into the washtub and set the jug down. Vina was downstairs in the living room, listening to a gospel choir on the radio and cracking her way steadily through a bag of English walnuts, her feet up on a stool. Earl and Ruthie and James were all asleep for once, her daddy sitting out on the front porch. Like he used to do, before her mama had died, she thought with a pang that surprised her after all this time. The two of them would sit out on the porch together in the dark, their voices soft, the swing creaking a little. Now, she knew, he was likely already drunk. As if, the thought came to her, he was trying to drink away this mess he'd brought on them all, as if he could forget her mama.

Her mama's image came clear—standing in this very bedroom.

"You open the window for us, Little Ann. My, don't that air smell good coming in like that? Here, you do the pillows and we'll have this bed made up in no time."

Like her mama had taught her, she'd opened and aired the second summer bedroom out this morning, put fresh sheets on the old featherbed, and swept the room out. The door had a wide gap at the bottom where leaves from the old pear tree might blow in or a squirrel or more likely a field mouse might scurry in. She wasn't scared of a mouse. A little mouse wouldn't hurt her. After supper and the little ones put to bed, she had heated the water for a bath and carried it jug by jug upstairs to a washtub in the bedroom. There was just the dresser to push across the door, and then she'd be able to bathe in peace. It's why she'd chosen to open up the second bedroom off the upstairs porch. The first bedroom held mostly sacks and boxes that Vina had brought with her—none of it needed in place of her mama's quilts and things.

Here in this room, at least for the summer months, she could get away from them all at the end of the day. The room wasn't heated, so it couldn't be used when the weather turned cold. But for now, it would be hers. Somewhere no one would be traipsing up and down all night, falling on the stairs, out of the crowded room she shared with Vina's three little ones, somewhere just to have a space to be alone. She took a deep breath as she gave the bed a final look of approval. Her eyes narrowed. The quilt was rippling slightly where it lay over the pillow. Catching her breath, she took hold of the corner of the quilt and flipped it back, afraid of what she would find. Her heart thudded against her chest, but before she could move, the bedroom door swung open and thudded against the wall.

Whirling about, she nearly choked at the sight of Estil leering at her.

"Go on, take off that dress and git in the tub. I'll wash your back for you." His eyes roamed across her body, and his low laugh made her skin crawl. She took one step back against the bed.

"Ain't no place to run and nobody to care, Little Ann. Your daddy's too drunk to know if you make a fuss. And my mama never begrudged me a bit of fun." He took one step forward. "I'm gonna make you pay now for stickin' Poke with that knife that time. You gonna take that dress off? Guess I'll just have to do it myself."

As he lunged away from the door towards her, she turned and snatched up the black snake that had been coiled under the quilt on her pillow. She whirled about, flinging the snake in Estil's face. The black snake coiled about his neck and struck at him.

"Ahh! Aghhhh!" Estil screamed and screamed again as the snake struck at his face once more. Staggering and stumbling about blindly, he lurched backwards out of the bedroom doorway onto the second-story porch. He screamed once more as his heavy body hit the porch railing and overbalanced, toppling over the railing. Rushing to the rail, she saw his body twisted on the ground below, the black snake trapped by his weight.

Hurrying into the bedroom, she dragged the bed away from the wall. Her hands shaking, she reached in and brought out her mama's treasures which had lain hidden and safe all this time. Grabbing her Sunday dress, her change of underwear, and her winter coat and socks from the bureau, she thrust all but the coat into a bundle. Pulling on the socks and boots she'd taken off moments before, she shrugged into the coat in spite of the warm night and stepped to the door, listening to the racket that Vina was making below.

"God Almighty, my boy, my boy! Oh my poor Estil!" Her shrill voice ratcheted up another notch. "Help me, Walter Lee! Git yer head out of that jar of likker!"

All the younger ones were squalling at the top of their lungs, and a low moaning told her that Estil had survived the fall. Poke was nowhere to be seen. Snatching up her bundle, she fled downstairs, through the living room, through the dining room, and into the kitchen where she grabbed a flour sack dish towel to put her belongings in. Tying up the corners of her makeshift bag, she let herself out the kitchen door and headed for the lane. Rounding the post office corner, she was out of sight of the farmhouse and paused to catch her breath. The wailing and sobs carried on the early night air as she turned and ran as hard as she could down the lane, away. John and Nancy Jane would take her in at least for the night.

Chapter 8

peach orchard

Little Ann folded up the quilts which made her bed on John and Nancy Jane's sofa and a sigh escaped her. Her sister-in-law looked up from the cook stove where she stood stirring flour into the cast iron skillet full of crumbled and browned pork sausage as she prepared their morning gravy. Baby Henry John lay cooing in his cradle. Little Ann smiled.

"It's right good to see a smile on your face," Nancy Jane declared. "Don't you git to worryin' about staying over long with us. You been a big help to me, I'm not afraid to tell it." Her glance strayed to her baby.

"He's such a sweet boy." Little Ann set the walnut cradle her brother had made for his first child to rocking gently. Henry John gurgled and waved a fist at the lock of her hair that fell forward as she bent over the baby to straighten his covering. Not like Vina's three, she thought, who seemed to have been born with their mother's selfish, whining streak. She came to the stove, put a second cast iron skillet on a burner and reached for the bowl of eggs ready to be scrambled.

"And I've had time to put my feet up and just enjoy all that sweetness," Nancy Jane told her, "with you here. But you ain't going to be a drudge, doing all my own work while I sit on my fanny and listen to the radio. That's not how I was raised!" Her sister-in-law paused to pour milk into the gravy, and stirring quickly, took the pan from the burner as the gravy thickened. Little Ann scraped the finished eggs into a bowl and set them on the table.

"We just got to think what you can do." Bending, Nancy Jane took the pan of browned biscuits from the oven. "You might call the menfolk in. Breakfast is ready."

John sat holding his son, the baby cooing and gurgling as his daddy tickled him, while Nancy Jane pushed back her plate. Peter helped his sister clear the table. "Jasper's the smartest dog in Lawrence County." The boy carefully lifted the stack of plates from the table with both hands and set them on the drain board. "John says so."

"Is that right?" Her little brother nodded. "He sure is one handsome beagle." Peter beamed.

A loud knock sounded at the door. John exchanged a look with his wife and handed her the baby. Rising, he gestured for the others to stay back. Through the opened door, she saw her daddy standing on the porch.

"I've come to git Little Ann," she heard him say to John.

"Well now, Daddy, that'll be up to her, won't it?"

"Now you listen to me," Walter Lee began, rocking back on his heels.

"Don't go," Peter whispered to her. "Don't you leave us!" She patted Peter on the head and walked out the door.

"It's okay, John," she told her brother. "You go on in, I'll speak with Daddy."

John hesitated before he nodded and stepped inside, leaving the door slightly ajar as he went.

"Well, Daddy?"

Her father looked away for a moment, scowling at John's mule in the paddock by the barn, and then turned to her.

"You need to stop this foolishness, Little Ann, and git home where you belong. They's just too much work for Vina to do, what with taking care of the young-uns and all." When she said nothing, he went on.

"Estil," he swallowed and began again, "Estil's a cripple, thanks to you. He done broke his back and he's no help to me on the farm and his mama's got to look after him all the time like he's a baby."

A derisive snort escaped her. Like Estil had ever done a lick of work on the farm!

"You've no call to act like that, girl!" Walter Lee snapped. "Estil done tole us how he carried them jugs of bathwater upstairs for you and you whining how the water was too cold and threw that black snake at him out of spite! You oughta be ashamed of yourself!"

She wrapped her arms around herself, her hands curled in fists. She might have known how Estil would twist the tale to suit himself.

"He done no such thing, Daddy! I carried that water upstairs myself and that miserable cur followed me up there and threatened to rape me," she hissed. Her daddy stepped back and raised a hand to his face.

"If it hadn't been for that black snake, Daddy, who would've helped me?" Tears were running down her cheeks now. "Where were you, Daddy, when I needed you?" she asked, wiping at her face.

Her father took a deep breath and swallowed.

"Well, now, that's awfully harsh language, accusing your poor brother of such a thing. But no matter now, Estil's in no shape to bother anyone no more. And your mama's carryin' again and she just cain't do all the housework by herself and take care of them young-uns and Estil. You gotta come home with me. She needs you." He smiled at her. "I ain't one to brag on my own children, but you's always been my favorite, Little Ann, and you's a hard worker." He reached over to pat her shoulder roughly. "Now go on and git your things and I'll take you on home where you belong."

"Estil Jones is not my brother," she spat at him, "and my mama, as you well know, is dead and buried up on the ridgetop." As her daddy's features contorted with anger and he reached to grab at her, the door was flung open behind them. John stepped out on the porch and put an arm around her shoulders. He glared at their father.

"You've said your piece, Daddy." He looked at his sister. "Well, Little Ann, what do you say?"

They were all gone, now, she thought numbly—Mama, Sarah, John, Martha, Alby, Peter, and Emmy and Emmett. She had no family left at home now—no one except her daddy. And here he stood before her—ready to drag her back to take care of Vina and the house and all the children the two of them could produce, no end in sight, and wait hand and foot on Estil to boot. With not one thought about Little Ann herself—about what she might hope for, dream about, if there were any dreams left to her.

She felt her brother's strong arm about her shoulders. Through hard work and his younger brother's help, John was providing for his little family. There was food on the table and the house was as snug as he could make it. But another mouth to feed, indefinitely? And what about when he and Nancy Jane added to their family? Where would there be room for her then?

John shook his head as if he could read the sense of hopelessness rising from her.

"You can stay here as long as you need to. I'm grateful for the help you've been to Nancy Jane and for the company you give her. It's a might lonely up here in the holler with no neighbors close."

She faced her daddy.

"I love you, Daddy," she told him, "but I ain't coming back. That place ain't been a home to me since you brought that woman there."

Tight-lipped, her father stared from his daughter to his son standing tall beside her.

"One of these days, missy, you'll be sorry you turned your back on your poor old daddy like this. And don't you come crawling back when you end up with nothing, either. 'Cause ever' thing I have, I'm leaving to my fam'ly what loves me." He turned without another word and stomped off the porch.

Brother and sister watched as he strode out to the road and away down the holler without a backwards glance.

John heaved a sigh.

"It's the likker, I guess. Daddy ain't the man he used to be. When he lost Mama....," his voice faltered to a stop and he shook his head. "Come on, let's go in. Nancy Jane will be happy to know you ain't leaving us just yet." He managed a grin.

Supper had come and gone, the dishes washed and the baby fast asleep, when another knock came at the door. John was in the barn with his brother at his heels, finishing the chores. Nancy Jane gestured for Little Ann to stay put where she sat mending one of Peter's shirts.

Her sister-in-law opened the door a crack, before swinging it wide to reveal Will Short on the porch. He held a covered bucket in one hand.

"'Evening, Nancy Jane," he addressed his cousin hurriedly. "Mama said I was to bring this berry cobbler to you'uns while it was still hot. She baked two tonight, she had so many berries from that patch along the fencerow by the barn." He thrust the bucket at her. "And I'm to tell you Mama said for you to bring that baby of yours to visit her soon."

"Come in, Will, and thank your mama kindly for us." She turned to Little Ann. "Mmm, this cobbler smells so good! Would you and Will run down to the barn and tell John and Peter to come to the house? I hear the baby fussing a little." She had her back to her cousin and winked at Little Ann as she set the bucket on the table. "I'd better see to the little master before he starts squalling."

The second time Will Short appeared on the porch bearing another gift, it was two weeks' later. This time he carried a small terracotta flowerpot holding a start of a deep purple African violet.

"This is for you, Ann." He held the potted flower in both hands. "Mama says ever' home should have something that blooms. This here's from a start my granny gave Mama when she and Daddy married." A fierce blush bloomed on his cheeks and he looked down at the deep purple blossom he held.

She felt something inside her shifting, warming, as she took the small flowerpot from Will. Something like wonder, that so small a thing could bring her this sense of hope.

"Thank you, Will. And tell your mama I surely appreciate her sharing her African violet with me. It's beautiful. I'll take good care of it."

Will looked up.

"I was wondering if you'd care to take a walk with me, Ann? We could go as far as the peach orchard and be back in plenty of time before dark."

"Let me find someplace to set this pot, Will, and tell Nancy Jane where I'll be."

Chapter 9

redbud

Little Ann lay abed in the front bedroom as light filtered in from the morning sun and slowly eased the chill as colors emerged from the gray muzziness that marked the predawn hours. The bedroom door opened; her grandmother came in with a covered tray. The smell of coffee filled her nostrils and she turned her head away.

"You've got to eat something, honey," her grandmother patted her hand, "and get your strength back. I've made you some oats and Poppy's brung you an orange from the store at Blaine."

Closing her eyes, she let her mind drift away from her grandmother's cajoling voice. Her grandmother and Poppy had come to stay for her lying-in, her first. Will had welcomed them, as anxious as she was for their first-born to arrive, especially with the baby coming early. And come the babe had, after six hard hours of labor. A little girl, Jenny Ann, Will had insisted, after her mama. With a head full of auburn curls and a sweet upturned nose, perfectly formed at six pounds, all her fingers and toes delicate. Perfect in all ways, except that baby Jenny Ann was stillborn. No cry of surprise at her moment of birth, no clucks of delight from Doc Carter or her grandmother, no hungry suckling.

She pressed her eyes tightly shut. She had not shed a tear. The grief was pressed into a dark, hard mass like a tumor where her heart should be, and she marveled bitterly that as yet she still lived, for it felt impossible that her heart was beating and her lungs still breathing in and out. Her mind drifted further afield. The sound of water running in the creek, flowing cold and swift over the flat, rounded stones in its bed reached her, filling her mind. Let the water carry her thoughts with it, she prayed, away from this cold room, cold house, cold heart. Listening to the creek, she fell asleep.

When next the light creaked beneath her eyelids and woke her, she discovered that she was lying on her side, facing the window onto the side of the porch that wrapped around from the front of the old farmhouse. Someone had come in while she slept, for the breakfast tray was gone and the curtains were pulled open. The window was shut against the early April chill.

After a while, she became aware that her daddy was out on the porch. He was sawing wood. She'd always liked to watch him at his woodworking, especially when he was making something, whether a rocker for her mama or a door for the henhouse. At such times, her daddy's face wore an expression that she sometimes saw on faces at church, intent and grave. All his movements were slow, deliberate, measured. Then the light caught his features as he turned his head. No, not her daddy. Her brother, John. So like their daddy—like the Walter Lee before he'd married Vina Jones. Sometimes she wondered if her daddy drank so much so he could forget Jenny Ann, forget her mama, forget who it was he bedded now.

She lay in her bed and watched as John sawed and sanded, running his finger around the edges of each piece he cut and sanded to make sure not a sharp edge remained. Only then did he fit the pieces together. Now he was brushing every last bit of sawdust from the tiny box. When he was satisfied that it was clean, he began fitting cotton batting to the bottom and sides and the underside of the perfectly fitted lid. His hands, so large and rough from untold hours in the fields and sawmill, deftly, expertly covered the cotton with a deep red satin lining. He held a tack with his lips as he secured the lining in place.

Never once did he pause or stop for a break, but worked steadily until the sun was slanting across the windowsill and sliding across the quilts of her bed. Only when his task was completed and his tools gathered up, the porch swept free of sawdust, did he stop. Little Ann watched as her brother stroked the tiny coffin gently and then nodded once, sharply.

A shadow darkened the bedroom doorway, and glancing up, she saw Will, his gaze stricken as he stared at John's handiwork.

"Oh Will!" Little Ann reached out a hand and her husband knelt beside her bed. Hands linked fiercely, tears slipped down both their faces. Head bowed, Will choked out a whisper.

"I'm so sorry, darlin'. She's so beautiful, so perfect! Why couldn't God let her live?"

Sarah set her large black handbag on the table next to Little Ann's bed and leaned over to peck her sister on the cheek. She made no move to hug her, but turned to drag a straight-backed chair up close to the bedside and sat.

"Winfrey and I were right sorry to hear of your trouble, Little Ann." Her sister fingered the thick string of pearls at her neck while her eyes darted about the room, taking in the flour sack curtains at the windows, the quilts on the bed, the water pitcher and basin on the washstand, and the faded hooked rugs on the floor. "We're staying in town, as we knowed you wasn't up to having company."

Sarah rummaged in her handbag a moment, before pulling out a small package wrapped in tissue paper. This she held out to her sister. "For you, Sissy." The old endearment slipped out unnoticed by Sarah, and Little Ann's hand shook as she took the gift.

Beneath the tissue paper was a pair of china salt and pepper shakers. The pattern was Blue Willow.

"Thank you, Sarah," She grasped her older sister's hand. "And thank you for coming."

Sarah gave her hand a slight shake and sat back in her chair.

"I thought you'd like them. You always did admire Mama's Blue Willow dishes." Her sister looked around the plain bedroom and her mouth tightened. "Just don't be like Mama, Little Ann. Don't wear yourself out having babies."

"Jenny Ann was our first, Sarah," she met her sister's gaze, "and Will and I both wanted her."

Sarah shifted on her seat.

"Winfrey and I, now, we've decided that raising the twins like our own is enough children. Why, Emmy's growed to be such a pretty little thing! She sings in the church choir every Sunday and Winfrey does love to spoil that child. He's paying a dollar a month for her to get piano lessons. You should hear her play!" Sarah shook her head and patted her curls back into place.

"Emmett gets more like Winfrey every day. Always has his nose in a book and writes a fine hand. They wanted to come see you, but we left them with Cora Mae. You know, Winfrey's cousin? She's the one you may recall who went to the teacher's college there in Morehead. Her husband Frank caught the influenza that winter it was so bad. Poor soul...."

She closed her eyes and let her older sister's words wash over her.

Walking carefully, Little Ann made her way in the fading light to the old cellar built into the hillside at the back of the farmhouse. John had sent a peck of apples last fall when she and Will moved into the old Caudill place. The neglected farmstead lay alone up a holler off a little intermittent branch of the south fork of Brushy Creek. Green and Josie Caudill, both in their eighties, had lived at the old farm alone, their daughter married and settled up north near Waverly, Ohio. The old man had been senile and a half-dozen years earlier he'd gotten out of the house in a snowstorm. Little wizened Josie had followed her husband's footprints. It was Josie's cousin, taking up their mail three days later, who found them both, frozen to death, ten feet apart near the gate by the road. The farmhouse had sat empty ever since, and their daughter had been more than glad to let them rent the place for no more than the yearly tax.

The thought crossed her mind as she wrapped her old coat closer, it was a wonder that Sarah had made the trip all the way up from Brushy into this God-forsaken holler to see her. But she didn't want to think of that time. She rested her head against the cellar door for a moment. Will had stored the apples in the cellar for keeping. There might be enough left to make baked apples to go with their supper of cornpone and milk. She would use the last of the sugar and cinnamon that Nancy Jane had given them as a wedding present when her sister-in-law and John stood up for her and Will at the courthouse in Louisa nearly a year ago now.

A sigh escaped her. She was so tired still, ever since they'd buried baby Jenny Ann up on the ridgetop next to her namesake. Nights like this seemed to come more often; Will's crops hadn't done well and there wasn't much work to be had at the sawmill near Blaine. When the flour and cornmeal ran out, she didn't want to think what they'd do then. The kitchen garden had done a little better than Will's attempt at farming; she'd been able to can some green beans and a little corn. The potatoes hadn't amounted to more than a few bushels, though. Those were all gone, and the last three cans of beans she'd canned had spoiled. Now she hesitated; she hated the cellar. It was small, dark and cold and the door was hard to open. But she wouldn't have to go far into it; the apples were on a shelf just inside the door.

Putting her shoulder to the cellar door, she shoved as hard as she could and it opened inward with a rush. She stumbled and as she did so a copperhead struck from the shelf where the apples rested. A scream escaped her, and she dropped to her hands and knees as the snake struck the air again above her. Scuttling backwards out of the cellar entrance, she left the door open, got to her feet and ran back to the farmhouse.

Later, snug under the covers, she felt Will's arms tighten about her.

"I'm so sorry." There was a pause, his words came choking out, then pouring. "I cain't seem to do anything right by you, honey. Ever since...ever since we lost our baby girl, I just cain't see my way. I cain't even feed you right. If you hadn't been feeling poorly and stumbled when you opened that cellar door, I'd have lost you, too. God, I'm sorry." His arms tightened about her again and she felt his tears against her cheek. "I'll do better for you, I promise."

Chapter 10

apple pickin'

Harry Short, Will's uncle, kept his eyes on the road as the old pick-up truck rumbled across the dark, cobblestoned streets of Chillicothe, Ohio, a cigarette dangling from his left hand. He'd smoke it nearly down to his fingers, and then pitch the stub out the open window of the truck. Pretty soon he'd light another one. Little Ann let her head rest against Will's shoulder. She thought her husband must be asleep; he hadn't said anything for quite a while now, not since they'd left Waverly behind them. Harry shifted down and brought the truck to a stop at a red light.

"Mama," Harry spoke into the darkness, referring to June, his wife, "she'll have your place ready for you'uns. They's not big, them workers' houses old Mr. Otto provides, but they's clean. They'll be enough room for the two of you. They's other workers from back home there, too. Some with young'uns. Mama's got plenty of company while I'm at work and the young'uns ride the bus to school there in town."

It was the most Harry had said to her since they'd left the hollers of Brushy Creek and, indeed, Kentucky, behind. Harry and June and their two half-grown sons had moved as far north as they could get and not fall into Lake Erie, she thought sleepily. Harry had gotten work picking fruit in the summers and into fall—peaches and pears and apples in the orchards around the tiny town of Berlin Heights, Ohio. The owners of the orchards kept small cottages for their seasonal workers, and it was in one of these that she and Will would be staying. Will's mother had suggested that Will should call Harry. His uncle had not only spoken to his employer, but he'd left June and his boys in Ohio and driven south to bring them back with him.

"The pay is good, Ann," Will had told her the day after the copperhead had nearly struck her in the cellar. "We'll be able to save enough to come back home and git us a decent place where we can make a good living. We can raise our family like we want, the good Lord willing." Because she was tired of being hungry and tired of being reminded every day of her brother John on that porch, building the coffin for their beautiful baby girl, she'd reached out and squeezed his hand and told him yes, she'd go north with him to Ohio. And now here she sat, scrunched on the truck seat between Will and his uncle, in the dark of night, scared to death about what it would be like to live up north, away from home, away from all that was familiar and loved.

Little Ann lay in the bed and let the nausea wash over her, a cold cloth pressed against her forehead. She had felt the sick headache coming on this morning, as she cooked Will's eggs before he left for work. He'd looked at her pale face and stroked her hair.

"You go back to bed and rest, honey. I don't like to leave you feeling poorly." But they both knew that not to show up for work could cost him his job. He'd made sure she was in bed and brought the cold cloth to her, then picked up his lunch bucket and thermos of coffee. "Try to eat a bite of something. They's bread you can toast and butter and some of that good apple butter Aunt June give us last week. I'll git her to come over and look in on you." She nodded to show him she'd heard, then he pulled on his jacket and hat and left.

His aunt came in not long after the school bus rumbled up the farm lane to the row of cottages to collect the workers' kids. She listened to their voices as the children clambered aboard the bus and to the sound of the old bus rumbling back down the gravel lane, the driver shifting down as the bus reached the blacktop. June was as lean as her husband and nearly the same height, her black hair cut to chin length and pin-curled into soft waves. A cigarette dangled from one hand and the smell of the smoke turned her stomach. June saw her flinch and stubbed out the cigarette in an ashtray on the table. "Sorry, girl. Will said you was feeling sick." She moved to the sink, took two cups from the dish drainer that sat there, went to the stove and poured a half-cup of coffee for Little Ann and one for herself. "Here," she brought the cup to the bed, "sit up and see if you can drink a few sips of this. My mama gits these same sick headaches. She swears a cup of coffee helps her."

A couple of sips was all she could manage before her stomach turned and she retched. June used the washcloth to wipe her mouth, rinsed it in the sink and brought it back. "Well, girl," the older woman took her hand and shook it gently, "if I had to guess, I'd say you's carryin'. Does Will know?"

"No." She licked her lips and closed her eyes for a moment as another spasm of nausea shuddered through her. "I'm afraid, June. I'm afraid this baby....," she couldn't put her fear into words, as if the fear itself once named would doom her and Will to another hard loss.

The older woman took both of Little Ann's hands in hers. "You listen to me, girl. You need to take care of yourself, eat good—I seen how thin you was when you first come up here and you ain't put on an ounce since then, I reckon—eat good," she repeated, "and I'm going to tell that husband of yours to have you see the doctors there in Huron. Lucille—you know Lucille and Hank Spradlin, don't you?" She continued at Little Ann's nod, "she lost two babies in a row back home, then they moved up here like we did and those doctors took good care of her. You've seen them kids of hers—ornery as little mules, them three is, and never sick a day in their lives. They's two doctors in the practice together—both of them are good doctors. You won't find no better up here."

Dr. Hoffman's office and waiting room sat at the front of the house where he lived with his family. His gray hair was neatly combed and from the moment he sat down in the examining room, wiry and calm in his white coat and spoke to her, she felt safe. He echoed June's advice to her.

"Take care of yourself, Mrs. Short, and you'll be taking care of your baby as well. I want you to make sure you eat healthy foods, get some moderate exercise—no heavy lifting—no alcohol, no smoking." He prescribed vitamins for her, which tasted awful, but she took them as ordered. The little grocery store in Berlin Heights carried fresh meat, milk and cottage cheese, prune juice when her advanced pregnancy brought constipation with it, and oranges and grapefruit later in the season. Will wouldn't let her mop the floor or even carry the wet laundry out to the clotheslines to dry. And when her water broke, early one evening, he borrowed his uncle's truck and rushed her to the hospital in Sandusky, where, with Dr. Hoffman attending, Deborah Ann Short was born at 2:07 a.m., kicking and squalling at the top of her lungs.

Bessie Smith was a bull of a woman and just about as agreeable; her hair was steel gray, the curls so rigid they might have been made of steel, it seemed to Little Ann. The librarian wore her glasses on a chain and they rested on the large shelf of her bosom when not in use. Her eyes were sharp as bits of coal and they followed every creak in the hard wooden floor as Little Ann walked to the adult section of books and pulled another Zane Grey western from the shelf. When Deborah Ann napped and with Will at work, she found there was time on her hands—the tiny cabin they occupied took no time to clean and straighten after Will left for the day's picking. June and Lucille came into town once week to do their grocery shopping and stop for a coke at the drugstore counter. June's older cousin Ermie, whose husband also worked for the Ottos, watched the babies and children too young for school so the other wives could do their shopping. Little Ann had noticed the public library the first time she'd joined the women on their shopping trip into town, leaving Deborah Ann cooing in her basket on Ermie's table. She'd braved the librarian, who made it clear without saying a word what she thought of Mr. Otto's workers and their families, and asked for a card so she could check out a book.

Now the librarian picked up the book Little Ann had placed on the counter and opened it to the back, where she stamped it precisely in the center of the next line on the due date card at the rear of the book. And before she grudgingly pushed it back across the counter, she repeated what she told Little Ann every time she'd checked out a book for the last month and a half.

"This book is due back in one week. One week. The fine for an overdue book is two cents per day."

"Yes'm." She could feel the librarian's eyes boring into her back as she left the library. At the post office, she collected their mail and found letters from her Grandma Emeline and Nancy Jane. The two of them wrote weekly and reading their letters was like a visit home each week. She swallowed a sudden lump in her throat and waved at Lucille and June as they emerged from the drugstore.

Back in her cabin, with the baby fed and down for her afternoon nap, she sat down to read her grandmother's letter.

Dear Little Ann, her grandmother began, *I hope this letter finds you and that baby of yorn and Will all doing fine. I am sorry to have to write and tell you this, but it is better you know what is going on. Your sister Martha never once gave Poppy and me a moment's trouble since she came to Louisa to live with us and go to high school. We was glad to have her. You know she got a job clerking at the Five & Dime store after she graduated high school? She went to church regular and every Saturday afternoon to the movie matinee with her friend Gladys. About a week and a half ago, one of those tent revivals was held at the church for a whole week. I went one time, but the heat was too much for me. I cain't say that I thought much of the preacher they had leading the revival. Del Simmons, his name is, and I thought he was a little too slick in calling the women up to be saved. But Martha said the singing and the praying was a wonder and she went ever night after work with Gladys. Well, the revival ended last Saturday night, and Sunday morning I found a note that Martha left for me on the kitchen table. She done run off and married that preacher, that Del Simmons. She were old enough not to need permission and they got married at the courthouse over in Johnson County, because old Miz*

Mason, the clerk there, rung me up and told me that she seed Martha right after the Justice of the Peace married them two.

I guess she will be traveling with the revival to wherever it goes, but I am sorely afraid, Little Ann, that your sister will be sorrier than glad. I don't trust that man, preacher or no. If you hear from Martha, will you write to me and let me know how she is? I have not heard a word from her except for that note she left me. Well, that is my news, I pray the good Lord will look after you all and hope to see you soon.

All my love,

Grandma Emeline

She read her grandmother's letter through a second time. Her grandmother was usually right about people. And her sister knew it as well as she did; that would be why she'd run off the way she did. Little Ann hadn't seen much of Martha once she'd moved to Louisa to go to high school. Her sister had found the town kids intimidating at first, but her schoolwork was more than a match for any of them. She'd done well enough to think about going to Morehead College after high school, but there hadn't been any money. She sat a moment, thinking—her sister had gone out with a couple of boys in high school and been invited to a few well-chaperoned dances. The only boy's name she could recall was Herman Pack; she thought he'd played football, but there hadn't been any romance to speak of between the two. Martha had told her sister, on one of their rare visits,

"Herman's just a friend. Anyways, he's like to spend his whole life right here in Louisa. When I finish high school, I sure hope to see more of the world than this here town!"

Although Grandma Emeline hadn't said so directly, reading between the lines, she had the impression that Del Simmons was likely a good bit older than Martha. Why had he married her? Her sister was a good-looking young woman; she had the black hair of her Sanders' kin and unblemished skin, blue eyes, and curves in all the right places. But she wouldn't bring any money with her, except maybe if she'd been saving part of her wages from the Five & Dime. Grandma Emeline, widowed now, lived on her small monthly government check. And the house, well, if Del Simmons thought he could get his hands on that, he'd better think again. When Grandma Emeline's time came and she passed away, Sarah wouldn't give so much as a penny from the sale of that property to any of her siblings, let alone to some sweet-talking traveling preacher.

She sighed and put the letter away. Martha was surely going to see more of the country than Louisa, Kentucky, if that was one of the reasons why she'd run off with that preacher. It seemed unlikely that she would hear anything from her younger sister. All she could do was pray that Martha knew what she was doing and that her new husband would be good to her.

Chapter 11

whippoorwill

The Chevy had a few miles on it, but its green and white paint job shone in the late autumn sun. Will wiped a speck of dirt from the passenger side door and opened it for Little Ann.

"I got a good deal on this car." He grinned at her and ducked his head, shutting the door for her as she settled Deborah on her lap. His brown curls fell forward as he climbed in the driver's seat. "Let's take a little spin so you can see how she rides. We'll be going home in style, Mrs. Short!" He laughed, started the engine, turned the car around, and started down the lane. "Don't that sound good, honey? Going home?"

She looked out her window, watching the waves as Will drove east along the lake shore road. "It sure does."

The house had one bedroom down, opening off the dining room, and a large living room across the front. The kitchen was at the back of the house and a stairwell led up from the side of the living room to two tiny bed-rooms. A wide porch ran the length of the front and one opened off the back from the kitchen. A small barn, the outhouse, and a chicken coop were situated beyond the back yard—part of which contained a vegetable garden, cornstalks dried and sharp, bean vines curling in the wind.

Will swung his wife and daughter into his arms and carried them both up the steps, across the porch, and into the living room. A wood-burning stove sat on the hearth where a fireplace was closed up.

"Mr. Roberts left plenty of seasoned wood on the back porch, honey. And there's more in the barn ready to be used. I'll git us a couple of armloads in, we'll git the house good and warm for you and the little missy before you know it." He headed for the kitchen as he spoke. "I'll bring our things in from the car when the fire's going good."

Deborah held onto her mama with one hand and looked about, squirming to get down. Little Ann jiggled her up and down and walked over to the window that overlooked the porch. The windows were tight; no cold air seeped into the room. Will was right, once the wood-stove was fired up—as well as the cook stove in the kitchen, she added to herself—the house would warm up in no time.

Mr. Roberts had been eager to sell the farm. It sat close to the dirt road that led back to Route 32, and when the road was good, it was an easy drive to either Blaine or into Louisa. He was a second cousin to Will's mother, widowed recently, with one son, who lived on the west side of Columbus up in Ohio. His son made good money in the factory where he worked as a maintenance man and had built a new house recently for his wife and their two kids. He'd made sure there was a large bedroom for his folks and there was enough land to the lot where he'd built for a garden. When his mother passed away unexpectedly, he and his wife had packed up his dad after the funeral and brought him home with them.

She ran her hand over the back of the couch. Much of the furnishings had stayed with the house. Mr. Roberts' daughter-in-law had gone to the furniture store and picked out new bedroom suites, new living room furniture, and a new dinette set for her new home. After all, she worked the night shift same as her husband. The only things they took from the homestead were a walnut secretary, a roll-top desk, and a collection of milk glass dishes. What was left was old maybe, but clean and well cared for. She had her own bedding and dishes, and carefully packed in the backseat of the car was a bassinet for Deborah.

Standing in the kitchen, she stared out back, lost in thought as Will whistled in the living room. When the ground thawed in the spring, she would get the garden cleaned up. And that was a rosebush she'd spied at the corner of the front porch, and a big old lilac out back by the clothesline. And before it got too cold, she'd gather the black walnuts littering the ground near the barn. She'd take the time to pound off those outer husks, and then spread the walnuts upstairs in one of the bedrooms to dry so they could be cracked as she needed them. A memory came to her, of Peter sitting on the post office steps next to her and talking about cracking walnuts with Mama. Sweet Peter! He was almost as tall as John now, Nancy Jane had written, and skinny as a rail, and his best friend was still his beagle Jasper—the smartest dog in Lawrence County. She smiled. She would have them all over for supper once they were settled in good.

Will slipped up behind her and wrapped his arms around his wife and child.

Christmas Eve the snow was drifted knee deep around the house and outbuildings. Will came in from the barn, stamping the snow from his boots.

"I gave old Elsie an extra measure of corn and made sure she's got plenty of water. I'll milk her in the morning while you git breakfast ready." He hung his barn coat on a hook by the door. "Umm, smells good in here, honey! Is that fudge you're stirring on the stove?" He came to peer over her shoulder.

"Yes, it is, and if you want to help, pour some cold water in the sink there. It's time to add the peanut butter and butter and the walnuts. Then I'll set this pan in that cold water and beat this fudge until it's ready to pour in the platter." She nudged him with her hip. "And if you're an extra good boy tonight, Mr. Short, I'll let you have a bite or two before Christmas Day."

He planted a kiss on her cheek. "Yes, ma'am!"

Fudge cooling and the kitchen cleaned up later, she fetched a glass of water from the sink and watered her

African violet. She'd repotted it since they'd moved back to Kentucky, and the plant was full of blooms. Picking up a tray with a plate of cookies and two cups of coffee, she turned out the kitchen light and moved into the living room. The Christmas tree stood in its bucket of water in front of the window, well away from the woodstove. Tinsel and popcorn strings and red and green paper garlands swagged the tree, the tinsel sparkling. Will came in from the bedroom, half-closing the bedroom door. He turned out the floor lamp by the couch, keeping the table light on next to the big armchair. He sat down and put his feet up on the ottoman. She set her tray down next to the table lamp, and he pulled her onto his lap.

"Deborah's sound asleep," he told her in a low voice. "I cain't wait to see her face in the morning when she sees all of this." He gestured at the Christmas tree and the stockings Little Ann had filled and hung from the tree.

"She's a little young to appreciate it, I think. But it sure is pretty." Under the tree was her gift to her husband, wrapped in brown paper and tied with a bit of ribbon. She'd sold butter she'd churned herself to the little store at Blaine after Will had taken some of their savings and bought Elsie the Guernsey cow from her brother. She'd earned enough money to buy Will a flannel shirt from the dry goods' store in Louisa. The blue and white plaid would suit him just fine. And there was the doll she'd sewn for Deborah. It wore a bonnet and a yellow flowered dress with a white apron. A contented sigh escaped her and Will hugged her close. It was the best Christmas she could ever remember, even if there wasn't anything under the tree for her. The house was warm and cozy against the snow-covered night beyond the windows. There was a ham with potatoes and sweet potatoes and cans of peas and green beans and corn to go with it. Along with the peanut butter fudge, she'd made a stacked apple cake and a pumpkin pie. Will had brought home a tin of Danish butter cookies and a bag of Spanish peanuts from the store in Blaine; they had oranges, too. What a Christmas feast they would have!

Little Ann sat at her quilt frames, her hands stilled, listening for the next cough. Spring had come late, with an ice storm in early April. And Deborah had begun to cough. The Vick's vaporub had seemed to help the child, along with the steam from a kettle of hot water with a towel over the little girl's head to help her breathe it in. She let out her breath and relaxed now, when no more coughs came. Old Doc Carter had retired before they'd moved back to Kentucky, and she'd heard nothing good about the doctors in town now. If only it would warm up, maybe then Deborah's cough would go away.

Looking down at her work once more, she threaded her needle and began a new fan of stitches in her quilt. She'd awakened on Christmas morning to find Will already up, the house warm, the coffee made. And under the tree, a long narrow package wrapped in sacking. "For you, Ann," he'd told her and watched her with anxious eyes as she opened his gift. The smooth poles, worn by years of use, the wooden ratchets that let the poles be tightened, the legs and braces made of two-by-fours. A quilting frame!

"Oh, Will!"

"It was Granny Short's, honey. Mama has her own set what Daddy made her for their first Christmas together. And she thought it would be fitting for you to have a set for our first Christmas in our new home."

She'd used the rest of her butter money to buy fabric at the store in Blaine. Through the rest of the winter, she'd pieced a quilt top, working on it evenings as Will listened to the radio and Deborah slept. Now it was up on the frame and it gave her something to do since it was too cold to start the garden. And something to keep her from worrying over Deborah's cough. And Will's restlessness. She didn't rightly know which worried her the most, although she tried her best to hide her thoughts from her husband. They had enough money saved, she knew, to keep them until the garden came in, so they wouldn't starve. But how was Will going to plant and work the fields on the ridge behind the house, or the little field to the side of the house? They didn't have a tobacco allotment, nor tractor, nor horse or mules to do the plowing. They'd have to buy seed to plant. Her brother had offered to bring his mules down when it came time to plant, but he had his own farm to work. Even with Peter's help, it was all John could do to get the work done there. And if it stayed cold like this and planting was late? So many things needed to fall into place. It would be all right, she told herself, it had to be. She loved the home they'd made together here. She loved being close to John and Nancy Jane, back where she belonged.

Milk sloshed from the pail as Will set it down on the kitchen table. Taking off his wet jacket, he hung it on a peg by the door. Without saying a word to her, he pulled out a chair and sat, his shoulders slumped. He ran a hand through his hair, then let the hand fall to his lap. Little Ann came to him then and knelt beside his chair, taking his hands in hers. And then he cried, reaching for her and pulling her onto his lap, wrapping his arms around her. When his tears stopped, they sat together, holding one another.

"I don't know what to do, " he whispered. "If I cain't git them fields planted, they's not going to be any corn to sell this fall. The money in the bank won't last long, and the manager at the bank turned me down when I asked him for loan to help us make it through until I can find work."

He tipped her face up to meet her gaze. "The only thing I can think to do, honey, is to go back north with Uncle Harry and Aunt June. I can work most of the summer and the fall and come home as often as I can to you and our baby girl. Save enough money to git us through another winter."

"No," she was already shaking her head before he finished. "If you go north, we'll be going with you."

"But, Ann," Will looked around the kitchen, "we cain't leave everything here and be gone that long. Well, I guess we could give Elsie back to John and Nancy Jane. Or," he paused, "we could sell this place and maybe find something with more bottomland when we come back."

In the silence which followed, Deborah began coughing, the cough soon turning into a thin rasping wail. Little Ann stood up and rested her hand against Will's cheek for a second. "Talk to Harry. We can sell up before we leave."

Chapter 12

buckeyes

Bessie Smith, the librarian, hadn't changed a bit. Not even the sight of Deborah, her dark curls bouncing, her blue eyes wide with wonder at the book with the colorful cover her momma lay on the counter, softened the woman's stern features. If anything, she stamped the back harder and seemed reluctant to hand over the picture book.

"This book is due back in one week. One week. The fine for an overdue book is two cents per day." She pushed it slowly across the counter to Little Ann. "And you'll have to pay to replace it if it comes back torn or soiled."

Deborah sat on the floor, her thin legs straight out before her, her book on her lap, turning each page carefully. June laughed.

"If I could get my wild ones to ever sit that still, it'd be a miracle!" She took a last drag from her cigarette and stubbed it out in the ashtray beside her coffee cup. "That little one's looking much better, girl. She still coughing?"

Little Ann brought her own cup of coffee to the table and sat down. "Dr. Hoffman says she's doing fine. She's just little, ain't never going to be big like me."

June laughed again. "That so? Then I reckon they all call you 'Little Ann' just to be contrary." She took a sip of coffee and sighed. "We done it, girl, me and Harry."

"What've you gone and done, June?"

"We've bought us a little house on the edge of town. There's a couple of acres and room to build us a new house someday. Harry says we can rent the little house to make the payments on the new house when we've saved enough. We ain't going back to Kentucky."

She smiled. "Well, June, I hope you'll come home to visit."

June laid her hand on Little Ann's. "You cain't keep us from visiting. But," her expression thoughtful, her eyes on Deborah, she continued, "the schools are better up here, much as I hate to say it, and the doctors, too, and, well, there's more money here. More work to be had." She finished her coffee and stood up. "We've thought long and hard about it all. Now, when you planning to tell that husband of yours that he's gonna be a daddy again?"

Sunday's dinner was fried chicken with mashed potatoes and gravy. Sliced tomatoes and green beans and a pone of cornbread rounded out the meal. Will pushed back his plate and sighed. "I swear, if I eat another bite of dinner, I'll pop! Don't tell her I said so, but your fried chicken's even better than my mama's." He brought his plate to the sink.

"Listen, honey, Willard Green's been talking to me about his cousin's place. You remember, it's up the holler a ways from them Caudills. It's going to come up for sale any time now, and Willard's made sure I can make the first offer. He says his cousin's a good man and the farm's in good shape. It's got a good bit of bottomland. Now, the house needs a little fixing up, Willard says, 'cause his cousin's been a widower for about ten years."

She let him talk as she picked up Deborah, wiped the little girl's face and hands, and set her on the couch with her book. Putting the remnants of their meal away in the refrigerator, she ran water in a kettle to heat for Deborah's bath and then filled the dishpan to take care of the dinner dishes. And all the while, all she could think about was packing everything up and setting off down Route 23 to Kentucky. And then packing everything up that they owned and heading back up the highway to Ohio once more. And coming back home again. And returning to Ohio. Harder and harder, especially with a child. Later, after Deborah had been bathed and fallen asleep, Will pulled Little Ann down beside him on the couch.

"Sit and rest, honey, you work too hard. Now, I'm thinking we should head home just as soon as Willard's cousin sells up. We've got enough money put by already to get us through the winter and to buy seed for spring planting, plus I figure we can get us a cow and some hens fairly cheap."

She pulled away from her husband and faced him. "You go on back to Kentucky if that's what you want, Will. Because, yes, I remember that place. It's in worse shape than where we lived when we was first married. You go on up that holler and live there if you want, but me and the kids are staying up here." Will frowned and she rushed on. "I'm tired, Will, tired of never being in one place long enough to feel like I've got a home. We almost lost Deborah, we would have if we hadn't come north when we did. June and Harry are staying here. Did you know that? June says the schools are better up here and so are the doctors and I know that for a fact." Her hand went to her abdomen. "And this baby is going to be born right here where we can have a good doctor look after us."

"A baby? We're having another baby?" Will's face lit up with a broad smile. He took her hand and pulled her back down to sit beside him. "When? When's the baby due? We can stay here and have the baby, then head home, honey." As she shook her head and started to rise, he pleaded with her. "It'll be different this time, I know it will." She shook off his hand and stood.

"I'm not going."

"How're you going to stay up here and raise two kids on your own? Tell me that." He was angry, rising to face her, fighting to keep his voice low and not wake the sleeping child.

"I'll find work, there's places hiring women. Ermie will watch the kids for me. I'll find me a place to rent. I mean it, Will. I'm not going back to Kentucky again."

Will turned on his heel, grabbed his hat from a nail by the door, his car keys, and let himself out. At least, she thought, hugging both arms about her thin frame to still the sudden trembling of her body, he didn't slam the door on the way out. She sank down on the sofa, her head in her hands and realized that she meant what she'd said. Whatever it took of her, she and her children were staying put.

He came in the next morning, took his lunch pail from the table without a word to her, and left again. Miserable, she wiped her face before Deborah could notice her tears and went through the motions of tidying the small worker's cottage. Maybe old Mr. Otto would let her pay rent to stay here this winter—at least until she could find something bigger. Around noon she took Deborah outside to play; a quick glance told her that Will had taken the car and left. He didn't drink much, so he wouldn't have headed out to a tavern. Maybe one of the men had needed a ride into town.

She had taken the meatloaf for supper out of the oven when she heard the door open. Will hung his hat on the nail and set his lunch bucket down on the floor by the door, then he came to her and wrapped his arms around her.

"You sit down, honey. You ought not to be doing too much in your condition. Let me wash up. I got a lot to tell you."

He served her a plate of food and set his own plate down before taking Deborah on his lap and cutting a slice of meatloaf into small pieces for his daughter. As the toddler picked up a bite of meatloaf and stuffed it in her mouth, he met her gaze. His mouth twisted for a moment.

"You mean more to me than any old farm in Kentucky, Ann. When I saw you that day at the dinner on the ground, I was plain struck dumb by the sight of you sitting there by your grandma. I knew right then I was going to marry you." He swallowed hard. "So I've done it, honey. When I took my lunch break, I went into Huron and got me a job at the feed mill there by the river. I'll be working the night shift, but it's a full-time job and I start in two weeks' time. I tole the man I wanted to be fair to Mr. Otto, and he was agreeable. And that'll give us time to find us a place to stay. A place with room enough for you and me and little Deborah and that baby when she comes."

Little Ann was laughing, tears sliding unheeded down her face. "When *she* comes? You got the sight, Will Short? What if this one here's a baby boy?"

He reached across the table to take her hand. "You wait and see if that baby ain't a girl. But won't we have some fun making us a couple of boys to go with them girls?" He was laughing now as she blushed.

Chapter 13

lilies

The Childers and Sloane Funeral Parlor, like many such establishments, had once been a fine two-story home in Louisa. A broad porch ran the width of the front of the building and curved along one side. On a warm day like this in early June, peony bushes hung full of blowsy pink blooms along both sides of the walk leading to the front steps. The funeral home was situated on a side street, only a few blocks from downtown Louisa and the Country Comfort Inn—the only hotel Louisa boasted.

Little Ann had chosen to walk from the hotel. Ahead of her, Deborah and Carole walked on either side of their Aunt Martha. Carole Martha Short was born three months after Will and Little Ann had moved into their first Ohio home, an old but sturdy farmhouse rented on the other side of town from his uncle Harry's place. And a few years later, after John William and David Henry made their appearances, with barely eleven months between them, Will moved his family into their own home. John and David—both still in school, had stayed home with their father. Watching Martha with the girls, she smiled. Her younger sister had had the good sense to divorce her traveling preacher husband once she'd had a taste of what being married to Del Simmons meant—always standing behind him, collecting alms, washing her laundry in a motel sink. Taking the slaps and berating when the good Lord didn't provide enough money. Looking the other way when Del put his arm around some little woman in need of counseling and disappeared for the night. Now she lived not far from Louisa in a snug little house on a couple of acres of land. Her second husband, Herman Pack, drove a truck across the country and Martha and their little Chihuahua mixed pup traveled with him as often as not now that their two boys were out of high school. Herman had been married and divorced before Martha came home to Louisa after divorcing Del. Herman's first wife hadn't been much interested in making a family or a home with Herman. She liked going out, dancing and drinking, and found plenty of men willing to do just that—unlike Herman. According to her grandmother, Martha hadn't been home a week when Herman came calling. They'd been together ever since.

On the porch of the funeral home, her brother John's firstborn held his baby daughter in the crook of his arm, a smile on his face as he listened to the man beside him. Surely that couldn't be James Lee? But then, he looked so much like his brothers—Earl, then Edward and was it Fenton? She had a hard time recalling her youngest half-brothers, but she thought Edward had been born shortly after she'd run away from home. And Edward had been followed by one or was it two girls and surely Fenton had been the last?

And there was Nancy Jane, hugging Martha and her girls in turn, her attention already half on Little Ann as she mounted the steps to the porch. Nancy Jane embraced her sister-in-law and held on tightly for a long moment.

"Lordy, Little Ann," the old nickname slipped out as though time had stood still and she was still that young girl running as hard as she could down the lane, away from the only home she'd ever known. "It is so good to see you!" Nancy Jane let her go and stood back as some of the children and grandchildren slipped out onto the porch. Through the opened doors she glimpsed rows of folding chairs set up in the front parlor, and beyond these, the open coffin where Walter Lee lay. John, looking so much like their daddy that she blinked, stood beside the coffin as the line of people shuffled through the receiving line to pay their respects.

She slipped her hand free from Nancy Jane's clasp with a murmur and stepped inside. She wrote her name in the visitors' book in the careful handwriting she'd learned at the one-room schoolhouse on Brushy Fork so long ago when Miss Hillis had taught them all. She took her place in line. Her thoughts skittered here and there, as if she could not hold them steady in the present. Vina had passed away near on ten years' ago, it must be. She hadn't come south on that occasion. But now, looking around, she could see Ruthie, the oldest of her father and Vina's daughters, holding court with a great gaggle of what must be her own children—the daughters as short and round as their mother and their grandmother before them. Somewhere in the crowd, she thought she recognized Earl's voice booming out.

"Oh yes indeedy, Daddy was right with the Lord before he passed. I baptized him myself just like in the River Jordan before my precious mama went to be with the Lord. Praise Jesus!"

Earl sounded so much like his older brothers, Estil and Poke, that she looked around for them before she could stop herself. Estil, she recollected, had died on the heels of his mother, and Poke—she had to think a minute. Hadn't Alby told her years ago that Poke had ended up in prison? Trying to rob the Liquor Mart in Fort Gay, that was it. Without Estil's support to keep him out of trouble, Poke had spent most of his time in and out of the Lawrence County jail until that armed robbery had sent him away for a long time.

The receiving line had moved along and now her older brother was reaching for her. John let her go reluctantly, looked away a moment as he took out his handkerchief. He turned with her as she approached the coffin that held her father's remains. The years of hard drinking, she saw, had taken their toll. Her brother, she thought and clasped his hand in hers, stood beside her as the image of the man their father might have been—had

Jenny Ann not died and left him. Vina had looked first and always to her own wants and needs, then to those of her ever-expanding brood of children. Walter Lee's well-being had never entered his second wife's mind, she felt certain. This man, this old man Walter Lee had become, had had no place in her own life—not since the night Estil had fallen from the upstairs porch and she'd fled with her meager belongings, the last of Jenny Ann's children gone from what had been their home—or in the lives of her children. Deborah and Carole had come to Kentucky because their mother had wanted to pay her respects to the father she'd once had. She bit her lip. She might as well have not come, she'd buried him the morning he stood on John and Nancy Jane's porch and turned his back on her. It was a wonder that it was John who stood by their father's coffin now, but for all his bluster, Earl wouldn't have the nerve to try and push him out.

Instead, Earl took the funeral service for his father, a side parlor filled with men and women from his church for when the hymns began. Earl began by reading the obituary which had been published in the *Big Sandy* newspaper. She brought her attention back to the service. Earl had grown up the spitting image of Estil, she thought, her lip curling. There seemed to be nothing of their daddy in his looks. Earl was now reading the list of survivors and she shook her head. Earl and Ruthie must have written the whole obituary—there'd been no mention of a first wife. Even in death, Vina had her way. And they'd forgotten Alby and Peter, but her younger brothers were nowhere to be seen in the crowd. Peter still lived with John and Nancy Jane, and Alby lived in Ashland now, with a woman who was a nurse. The names of Alice and Alvin threw her for a moment, until she realized they were meant for the twins. As far as she knew, Emmy and Emmett had never been back to Brushy to see their daddy since they'd gone to Louisville to be raised by Sarah and Winfrey. Emmy'd defied her sister Sarah when she was grown and had gone to nursing school instead of staying home to take care of the house and Sarah. Her older sister hadn't come to the funeral, not that she expected her to show up. Sarah had never spoken to their daddy since the day she'd married Winfrey and moved out of the house on Brushy. Emmett had followed Winfrey and worked for the railroad. The last she had heard from him, his twin girls were healthy and happy and his wife was a clerk in a lawyer's office there in Louisville. Now she realized the obituary had not included her name either. No matter, there were those who would remember Jenny Ann, would remember Walter Lee and his family before his second marriage.

Earl was preaching now, worked up in that shouting, barking manner that marked a United Baptist preacher, preaching how they all needed to accept Jesus Christ as their savior or suffer from eternal damnation. The brothers and sisters of his congregation called out "Amen" as the shouting reached its peak. Beside her, Deborah was jiggling her leg—a sure sign of the girl's impatience. Carole, on the other side of her older sister, leaned in close to whisper loud enough for her mother to hear, "Not a single word about Grandpa, not a single memory to share." Deborah snorted in response and Little Ann nudged her. Her daughter grinned, but her leg stopped jiggling.

Now Earl was thundering a prayer, asking the Almighty Lord to call all the sinners gathered there to repent. Then the singers launched into their first hymn. She had never enjoyed the droning version of singing that characterized the old-time Baptist church into which Earl had chosen to become baptized. Every hymn sounded exactly alike and no music was ever permitted to accompany the singers. A second hymn followed the first before Earl called the mourners to join him in a final prayer. It had been a fairly short service of its kind, it seemed to her.

Deborah drove her mother and sister to the cemetery. Walter Lee was laid to rest in the older portion of the cemetery just outside of Louisa, where he shared a headstone with Vina. Thankfully, the graveside service was equally brief—just a recitation of the Twenty-third Psalm. The mourners milled about afterwards, small knots of people forming, loosening, reforming. She paid them no heed. She wandered away to stand alone, arms clasped about her waist, staring off at the distant forested ridges, the hollows and streams hidden from view. This country, still after all these years, tugged at her heart and soul. Home. Ohio receded before these hills, these mountain valleys. Northern Ohio's tidy small towns, orchards, small industries, shops, schools, faded like a dream. Here, now, this land fed her roots, sustained her. Out there, a little farther south, Brushy Fork ran swift and cold at the foot of the curved ridgetop—as yet untouched by mountaintop removal—where her mama and baby Jenny Ann lay buried all these long years. And it seemed to her that all these years, too, she'd carried in her heart the man her daddy had once been. And now that image was gone.

From her side, Carole touched her arm.

"Mom? You okay?"

"I feel like an orphan." The words slipped out and Carole put her arm around her mother, turning her away from whatever it was her mother saw out there, whatever grief tore at her, making her look so lost and alone.

"Come on, Mom. Uncle John and Aunt Nancy Jane and Aunt Martha want us to go eat with them. Deborah's already said there's no way she's going to the hall at Uncle Earl's church."

"No," She put her arm around Carole's waist. "No, indeed. We'll eat, and then we'll head home."

For her daughter's touch had brought with it a clear image of home. Will would be on his way to work right about now, leaving the house closed and empty behind him. With their father working nights and their mother gone, her boys would be up the road, spending the night with Harry and June. She wanted, suddenly, to be there waiting when Will came in from work. She wanted to get home, get unpacked, pick up her boys, see them and the girls settled for the night. Maybe she'd have time to bake something. If she wasn't mistaken, there was a box mix for an angel food cake in the cupboard. And a can of fruit cocktail to go with the cake—Will's favorite dessert. She'd read a bit after the kids were in bed, maybe that new mystery Carole had finished, and stay up until Will was home.

"Umm, smells good in here!" As Will set his lunch bucket down on the countertop, she sliced the angel food cake and spooned the fruit over it. He took two cups from the dish drainer and poured them half-full of coffee. He set the cups down on the kitchen table, one to either side of the African violet blooming there. They usually ate their breakfast—and the rest of their meals, too—at the kitchen table if the kids weren't around.

"Thank you, honey," he said. His eyes were shining with the light of his smile, warm and full of love. He reached across the table and took her hand in his. "I'm glad you're home."

She would tell him, as they ate, about their trip down south and back, about who all was there at the funeral, about the meal she and the girls had shared with John and Nancy Jane and Martha. And he would smile at the thought of the little ones grown up now and shake his head at Earl's behavior and then he'd say, "Leave those dishes for me, honey. I'll wash up in the morning. It's been a long day, let's go to bed."

But she wouldn't tell him of the sorrow she'd felt, the sense of loneliness that had overtaken her standing there in the cemetery looking out over the hills and hollers of home. The way memories had ebbed and flowed around her. How she could feel the warmth of the bare wooden porch floor beneath her feet early summer mornings when as a child she'd slip out of the house and follow her grandmother to the hen house. The taste of her mother's strawberry jam on a fresh biscuit. Her mama's shy voice lifted in a hymn as they folded laundry. The scent of her daddy's tobacco as he squatted in the hay field and rolled a cigarette. Or her daddy drinking thirstily from a cold jar of lemonade her mama had sent out to the field. Sunday dinners, the tables set up out on the front porch, her grandparents and all the aunts and uncles and cousins the tables could hold laughing and passing around mounded platters of fried chicken and greens and potato salad.

It was that great web of memory and love that had kept her going during the hard years after her mama died, she thought now, after her daddy turned his face from them. And slowly, with care and hard work, she'd had a chance to weave that web around her life again. Here in this new place, this second chance, filled with family—with Will and their kids in this place they'd made their own. She squeezed Will's hand.

"I'm glad to be home."